RAVES FOR *WINTER MEETS SUMMER*

Christine Noyes excels in delivering a delightful and heartwarming romantic comedy with vivid characters and a story that beautifully balances humor, emotion, and personal growth.

Winter Meets Summer is an uplifting read that leaves readers with a renewed belief in the magic of love, no matter the season of life. Christine Noyes has crafted a touching tale of love, self-discovery, and the joy of embracing the unexpected.

—Natalie Soine
Readers' Favorite 5 Star

Winter Meets Summer is for fans of romance, drama, humor, and psychology. A witty and profound read, touching on questions about our place and true purpose in life.

—Nino Lobiladze
Readers' Favorite 5 Star

Winter Meets Summer is an ideal romance novel for fans of the genre.

—Diana Lopez
Readers' Favorite 5 Star

Christine Noyes proves once again her ability to make us fall in love with characters like they are our own family. *Winter Meets Summer* is a beautiful story of love, second chances, and the meaning of life. Beautifully written, it's nearly impossible to put it down once you pick it up. Five stars!

—Taylor Cournoyer,
human resources professional

Christine Noyes takes the idea of love—a concept that has been dissected by authors for eternity—and manages to make it inspiring again. She proves older love is simpler and yet more complex all at the same time. *Winter Meets Summer* made me laugh, cheer, and acknowledge that unconditional love is timeless.

—Brenda Anderson
administrative assistant, retired
Orange, Massachusetts, Police Department

WINTER MEETS SUMMER

Other Books by Christine Noyes

Memoir

Close Enough to Perfect

Fiction

A Picture of Pretense

Shadow in the Sandpit

Meet Your Maker

Children's Books

A Big Al Bear Hug

Big Al Helps Clean the Park

The Case of the Missing Cooler

Big Al's Treasure

Audiobooks

Close Enough to Perfect

A Picture of Pretense

COMING IN EARLY 2024

Pathside Predator

ChristineNoyesAuthor.com

Winter meets Summer

a novel

CHRISTINE NOYES

Haley's

Athol, Massachusetts

Haley's
488 South Main Street
Athol, MA 01331
marcia2gagliardi@gmail.com • 978.249.9400

Cover designed by Christine Noyes with licensed online images from Shutterstock and Unsplash.

Developmental editing by Rozi Doci.
Copy edited by Marcia Gagliardi.
Proof read by Richard Bruno.

International Standard Book Number, trade paperback:
    978-1-948380-99-7
International Standard Book Number, Kindle:
    978-1-956055-00-9

Library of Congress Cataloging in Publishing pending

For all those who have loved, lost,
and hope to love again.

I am who I am,

I am who I'm going to be,

I'm going to be who I am.

-Christine Noyes

CONTENTS

WINTER

TED

"I won't let you go," Ted Winter promised as he gazed into her hazel eyes. In her, he saw perfection. Her embrace soothed his weary body, and he determined to hold on to the moment. But in his weakened state, the intensity of the pull overpowered him, and he felt her slipping from his grasp. His fingers brushed her arm as she drifted away. Dressed in white light, she slid into the darkness. "Carol," he called. But she had already gone.

Ted awoke with a jolting pain and reluctantly opened his eyes. The overwhelming odor of antiseptic filled the air, and reality enveloped him like the starched white sheet tucked snuggly around his body.

"Ah, Mister Winter, you're awake. Good," the nurse said enthusiastically. "How do you feel?"

"Terrific. I'm ready to hit the links," he managed to say. Because his thoughts remained with Carol, he needed a minute to collect himself.

She's dead. The thought elicited a new pain in his chest. A few moments before, she'd been in his arms. Ted ran his thumb over his fingertips. He could almost feel her silky-smooth skin. It'd been years since she'd passed away, but the dream had felt so real. He wished he would have stayed with her.

"I'll let the doctor know you're awake," the nurse said.

Ted nodded silently as recent memories began to surface. He'd been at the office with his business partner Chip reviewing tax documents for a client when he felt a tightness in his chest. He vaguely remembered getting dizzy and hearing Chip say, "Don't you die on me, Ted." Then everything had gone blank.

His next recollection was lying in the ambulance strapped to a gurney thinking Alex was right. He was going to die.

Alex, the cook his daughter hired to prepare dinners for him after his first heart attack, may have been prophetic just three days earlier when he suggested Ted's death would likely be the result of his poor diet. When Ted had insisted on spaghetti instead of zucchini noodles, Alex had responded with, "Okay, it's your funeral."

My funeral? No, not today, he thought as he reached for the hospital bedrail.

Ted tried to sit up but couldn't muster the strength. He felt the mattress on either side of him as he searched for the remote control. Once he found it, he raised the head of the bed as high as it would go while wincing at the discomfort he felt in his chest. He swung his legs off the side of the mattress. After adjusting his hospital gown, he searched the floor for his shoes. Seeing nothing, he gingerly walked barefoot to the closet positioned just inside the door of his room. Empty!

"Looking for something?"

The familiar voice came from behind him.

"Where the heck are my clothes, Dan?" Ted asked as he looked into the empty closet.

"Your daughter took them with her. She had an inkling you might try to leave the hospital during the middle of the night."

"I might have if you hadn't slipped me a mickey."

"Nothing like a little morphine and oxygen to relax a weary body," said Dr. Daniel Parsons as he stood in the doorway with his hands in his white lab coat pockets. "Get back in bed, Ted."

Begrudgingly, Ted climbed back on the edge of the bed.

Ted's longtime friend pulled a chair next to him and sat. His expression grew serious as he looked up at Ted. "This was number two. Don't you think it's time to start taking your heart health seriously?"

"You really think this is the right time for a lecture? Shouldn't you be trying to boost my spirits or something?"

"The next one could be your last. No lecture, no bullshit, just truth. You've worn yourself out with excessive work and lousy eating habits. Isn't it obvious? I am no longer using the term if. I'm saying when. When your next heart attack comes, Marci may not have to steal your clothes to keep you from leaving."

"Jesus, Dan." Ted gazed at the floor as a full docket of emotions vied for his attention: anxiety, fear, vulnerability. The last one especially made him feel guilty, a product of his father's demands that he be strong-willed and impervious to his emotions.

"You can't put this off any longer," Dan said, breaking the short silence. "You need to drastically change your lifestyle. You're sixty-seven years old, Ted. Your body is telling you it's time to slow down."

"Look who's talking. You're a year older than me, my friend. And you're still working."

Dan sat back in his chair, crossed his arms, and lifted a brow. "They dragged me off the golf course when you had your heart attack. I only see a handful of patients anymore. Call it semi-retirement. And I take care of myself."

"Off the golf course, huh? Sorry about that."

"You should be. It was my first round of the year. I'd been looking forward to it all winter. And I had three birdies through the first five holes."

"All right. I get it. I'll slow down at work and eat healthier."

"I'm afraid that won't be enough, Ted. You've created an unhealthy routine, and you've refused to alter it. Look where that's gotten you. Your stress level is off the charts. You sit behind a desk all day getting little to no exercise. And, from what Marci tells me, your breakfasts consist of pre-packaged pastries and coffee. When I said you need to drastically change your lifestyle, I meant drastically. I recommend you never go back to your office again."

"Oh, come on, that's crazy. I have clients to take care of. I have responsibilities."

Marci walked through the door with Ted's freshly laundered suit in a plastic bag. "Chip can handle the law firm. You've been grooming him for years," she said. "Hi, Dan, is he giving you a hard time?"

"Did you have any doubt that he would?" Dan smiled and stood to give Marci a kiss on the cheek.

After hanging Ted's suit in the closet, Marci went to her father and wrapped her arms around him. They lingered in a hug for several moments before she drew away, wiped her eyes, kissed his cheek, and said, "Now, stop being a pain in the ass and listen to your doctor. Because if you don't, I'm going to pack up my husband and kids and move in with you."

Ted chuckled at the notion.

Marci glared at him without a speck of humor in her expression. "I'm not kidding."

"You wouldn't." Ted swallowed hard.

"Come to think of it, the schools are much better in your district. And I bet the acoustics in my old bedroom would be perfect for Casey to practice on his new drum set, which you bought for him."

"Ouch," Dan said as he cringed. "Remind me never to get on your bad side, Marci."

"Ted," said the doctor, "I'm keeping you here for a couple of days so I can monitor you. Then, if everything looks all right, I'll send you home. But if I hear you've stepped foot in that office of yours, my first phone call will be to Marci. Now I'll leave you two alone."

Ted softened his posture and his voice. "Hey, Dan. Thanks."

"Anytime," Dan said, then left the room.

"So, what's the plan?" Marci asked as she sat in the chair.

"Plan? What plan?" Ted asked.

"Your plan, Dad. What are you going to do to change your lifestyle? And before you speak, remember whatever plan you come up with will determine where me and my family will be living."

"Marci, Dan is overreacting. He does that. He's a doctor, it's his job. But I promise to slow down. I'll cut my work hours and eat zucchini noodles if that's what it takes."

"Okay," Marci said as she got up from the chair. "I'll pack up the kids and we'll be at your house by dinnertime. Frank will enjoy the short commute to work. Or you can move in with us."

"Wait. What?" Ted asked.

As she walked to the door, she replied, "It's obvious you aren't going to be a responsible adult and do what needs to be done. So, you leave me no choice."

"Wait. No, no, wait!"

Marci turned to look at him from the doorway.

Ted sighed. "I'll call Chip in the morning and make the arrangements. Maybe I can wrap things up from home."

"And?"

"And I'll let you plan my meals with my cook. Alex has been trying to get me to eat healthier for the last year. He'll be in bland-food heaven."

"That's a good start, but it's not enough," Marci said.

"Not enough? That's my entire life: my work and food. What else could I possibly give up?"

"I know you. The temptation to go back to the office is going to be too much. You need to get away from here. You need to take an extended vacation."

"Why would I need a vacation if I'm not going to work?"

"Because if you don't get away from here, you'll be thinking about work. If you're thinking about work, you might as well be at work. I've got some pamphlets in the van. We'll talk about it when you get home. Right now, you need to rest."

Marci gave Ted another kiss on the cheek and turned to leave. Ted stopped her.

"Wait a minute. Home? Which home are you referring to?" Ted asked.

"I guess we'll have to wait and see," Marci grinned.

BEING SUMMER

SUMMER

Summer removed her father's bedpan. The stench made her wish she'd skipped breakfast. She emptied the pan into the toilet, then placed the putrid potty on top of a brown paper bag she had spread on the bathroom floor. As she stood upright, she caught her reflection in the mirror.

Her long gray hair had begun to escape the elastic band she had used to bind it together before the sun rose. Sweat-filled strands flopped onto her face but did not conceal the dark circles under her eyes nor the loneliness within them.

"C'est la vie," she whispered, then chuckled at the irony of using the French language to lighten the moment.

Her memories took her to 2008, fifteen years before, and the trip to Paris she and her husband, Arnold, had planned. They had delayed the vacation multiple times due to Arnold's business obligations but had finally made hotel reservations and bought airline tickets. They never made it. Arnold had died of a heart attack two weeks before their scheduled departure. His death devastated her personally and threw her into a world she had, until then, carefully avoided—a world of contracts, business relationships, and publicity all while she fulfilled responsibilities of caregiver to her ailing parents.

She turned away from her reflection and walked to the end of the hallway where her bedridden mother lay. With the volume of the television tuned to its maximum, she could barely hear herself groan as she retrieved the bedpan. Holding her mother's excrement in the pan in front of her as if a ticking time bomb, she hurried back to the bathroom and began the cleanup process.

Summer always had a warmhearted but guarded relationship with her mother, Delores. They could never truly open up to each other, mostly because her father, Carl, harshly squelched any conversations of a personal nature. He believed showing signs of affection toward Summer equaled coddling her. The few tender moments she shared with her mother occurred after school in their kitchen before Carl returned from his job at the tool and die factory. Summer suspected her mother had learned early in their marriage what was expected of her. She cooked, cleaned, shopped, and doted on her husband as she was conditioned to do. Not until her teenage years did Summer recognize her mother's role in the marriage—to be dutiful and silent. And to bear the brunt of Carl's physical and emotional outbursts.

Carl cast his judgment on everyone around him. He often stated that his way was the only way. Pleasing him was as easy as emptying a bedpan into a soda can. It could be done, but it required a lot of patience and immense fortitude.

After washing her hands thoroughly, Summer moved to the kitchen to prepare her parents' mid day meals, one of the three menus her father would eat—puréed skinless hot dogs with a side of mashed New England baked beans.

I might as well have scooped out the contents of his bedpan and thrown it on the plate, she thought. Worried that someone may have eavesdropped on her thoughts, she unconsciously scanned the kitchen.

When Summer first started caring for her parents, she had suggested that, because of Carl's limited palate and her own desire to stretch her culinary muscles, she prepare a separate meal for

Delores. The comment caused an outburst. For hours after, Carl verbally degraded his wife and accused Summer of squandering his hard-earned pension. He had no idea that his pension barely covered the electric bill, but Summer had no intention of getting into a conversation with him about money. Later that day out of earshot of her husband, Delores pleaded with Summer to never mention nor entertain the idea of separate meals again. Summer honored her mother's request.

With the hot dogs whirring in her food processor, Summer glanced at her professional-grade cookware packed in a box in the corner of the kitchen. She had been living with her parents for nearly five years and still hadn't put it in storage. Hope sat in that corner—hope that she would again enjoy the art of cooking one day.

After lunch, Summer pulled a worn wooden chair to her mother's bedside, the same chair her mother used to sit on and knit. She reached for the book that sat on the bedside table. It was her mother's favorite story, *Little Women* by Louisa May Alcott.

"It's story time, Mom. Let's see what Jo, Meg, Amy, and Beth are up to today," Summer smiled and brushed a piece of hair from her mother's brow, stroking her head lightly.

She fanned the pages to the bookmark at Chapter 42 and began reading about Jo and her reaction to her sister Amy's engagement. A thin smile increased the wrinkle count on her mother's cheeks. The smile quickly faded as Delores fell asleep after only two pages.

It's okay if you don't make it to the end of the story, Summer thought as a tear rolled down her cheek.

Early that evening as Summer sat by her side, Delores peacefully passed away. After several minutes of tears, Summer dried her eyes and went to tell her father. But Carl lay lifeless on his bed, his body still warm to the touch.

Summer didn't understand her parents' relationship, but in that moment, she appreciated how strong their connection had been.

Four months later, holding a smoldering sage bundle lightly in her hand, she traced the door frame of her parents' small white cottage. Then, with a flick and a wave of her hand, she declared, "That's that," and turned her back on the past.

She rounded her pale yellow VW bus as she moved her arm in circles with the sage, creating her savory cloud of comfort. The vintage sixteen-foot Shasta camper tethered to the Volkswagen received the same thorough ceremonial cleansing. Only then did Summer step into her van ready to move forward physically and emotionally.

HOME AWAY FROM HOME

TED

As Marci drove the Massachusetts Interstate on the way home from the hospital, Ted fingered through the stack of pamphlets she had amassed. "A dude ranch? Marci, you can't be serious with this stuff. Why don't you have any pamphlets for nice hotels in New York, New Orleans, or New Zealand?"

"Dad, I've never seen you go into a hotel without giving at least three people your business card."

Ted picked up the next flyer and read, "Sleepy Pines Resort? Let's see what kind of gem this is." He flipped to the next page and continued reading. "Rustic cabins nestled in the foothills of the White Mountains."

"That sounds peaceful."

"Peaceful? Oh, honey. Rustic means old and drafty, and nestled in the foothills means the trees are growing out of the cabin's foundation and won't withstand the next mudslide that will undoubtedly overtake the scenic view and plunge the remnants of the cabin into the quaint, sparkling pond."

When Marci didn't respond, Ted looked up from the brochure and saw tears streaming down her face.

"Honey, what is it? Marci?"

"I don't want to lose you. I'm not ready. And I'm afraid that you don't want to put the effort in . . . that you're in too much of a hurry to be with Mom."

Ted's heart ached. After five years, losing his wife remained a fresh wound. Just as he felt life with Carol had defined who he had been—a happy, energetic, loving husband and father, life without her had also defined him. He lived in his memories. Ted buried himself in his work while ignoring his personal life—present and future. He preferred it that way, but he knew it wasn't fair to Marci. Not only had she lost her mother, but the father she once knew disappeared as well. As much as he tried for Marci's sake, he could not get that man to return.

"Sweetheart, I'm sorry. I wasn't thinking. Of course, I want to be here with you for as long as I can. It's what your mother would want, too. You and me, pumpkin. We're a team."

"Promise me you will take Dan's advice seriously. He wasn't overreacting, Dad. He was really worried this time. We all were."

Ted placed his hand on Marci's shoulder. "I promise."

For the next twenty minutes, they drove in silence.

Marci pulled off the highway and headed to her father's home in Newton. Ted had driven that road for thirty-five years but now, as a passenger, noticed things he had never seen before. The doggie daycare that boasted "Pet Reiki Appointments Available." The tattoo shop with skull and crossbones on its sign.

Phillips Hardware store looked old and accomplished, while Stuffy's Bakery recently updated its look with vibrant colors. The large sign above Brandon's RV & Services read "Your Home Away From Home." Brandon's had grown from a small, single-person operation to a large business that employed more than sixty people. Ted's firm had done work for them during their latest expansion.

"Your home away from home," Ted muttered.

"What did you say?" Marci asked.

"Nothing. I was just thinking out loud," Ted answered. But inwardly, Ted considered a possible solution to placate Marci.

Three days later, after exhaustive research into which brand would provide him the most comfort, Ted purchased a motorhome. Before he drove the forty-foot beast off the RV lot, he waited until there were no cars in sight. He gingerly pressed the gas pedal, but the vehicle did not move. He pressed harder on the pedal and still got no forward motion. Someone behind him beeped their horn.

Ted turned the wheel to the right and bore down on the gas. The RV lurched across three lanes of traffic-free roadway and climbed the median strip with the left-front tire before thumping back down into the marked lane. Ted's heart pounded as the traffic light ahead turned red. He slammed the brake. The motorhome abruptly stopped but propelled Ted forward—his seatbelt kept him from landing on top of the cockpit that surrounded his soft leather driver's chair.

His hands shook, and he took a deep breath. "Okay, it's just straight from here," he mumbled.

The largest vehicle Ted had ever driven was his sons-in-law's Dodge Ram pickup truck. He'd thought driving the Provost motorhome would be the same. He began to realize he was wrong.

The signal light turned green. With traffic then to his right, Ted incrementally eased the gas and inched forward. "Okay, this isn't so hard."

He stopped at several red lights before considering his shift to the right lane.

"Oh, bugger. Birch Street."

He pictured the street where he lived. The houses at the beginning of the street were old and provided only single car driveways. Most residents on both sides parked an extra vehicle in front of their homes, narrowing the travel capacity by almost twenty feet.

If I can make the right turn from the middle lane, the radius will be sufficient. But what can I do if there's traffic to my right? I'll have to deal with that . . . now.

Ted allowed the cars on the right to pass him then slowed the motorhome to just fifteen miles per hour. As he approached Birch Street, he flicked on his right turn signal. Ted began to turn just as the impatient man in the white Corolla darted out from behind him into the right lane. It forced Ted to slam the brakes, which jolted the motorhome to a dead stop and flung Ted forward only to be caught once again by his seatbelt.

Horns blared as Ted tried to regain his composure and ease the monstrosity onto Birch Street, carefully skimming by parked cars without incident.

He released the breath he had been holding.

Ted inched his way past the older section of Birch into the newer development built thirty years before. Ted and Carol had bought a new house after Ted landed a large account to seal his law firm's success. The home was the first luxury the two had allowed themselves and much bigger than they needed.

Carol had loved the home's entrance—each topped with electric lanterns, two concrete pillars flanked the driveway. One of Carol's first gardening projects had been adding decorative ivy to the columns. Since then, they'd grown to completely cover each pillar.

I thought a fifteen-foot-wide driveway was excessive. Now I'm not so sure.

He stared at the two columns.

"Okay, you've got this," he said. "Piece of cake."

Ted envisioned the turn radius and crept into the driveway. With the nose of the RV past the posts, Ted saw through the side mirror that the right edge of the vehicle would not complete the turn without scraping the pillar. He checked for traffic behind him, saw none, and backed out.

His second attempt brought him in a little further before he edged dangerously close to the ivy-covered post. Once again, he backed out.

Another attempt, another fail.

With each try, he felt more contempt for himself. Ted did not handle failure well, a lingering effect of his father's expectations. According to his father, failure in anything was not an option. So when Ted did have difficulty completing a task, it often spurred a sickly, physical reaction. He succeeded with his sixth maneuver and parked the RV in front of his garage.

I'm never getting into this thing again.

Once inside his home, Ted dialed Marci's phone. "Hi, Marci. I was wondering if you could give me a ride to pick up my car."

"Where is your car? Is everything all right? Did you have an accident? You didn't have an accident, did you?" Marci asked frantically.

"No, I didn't have an accident. I just need to pick up my car."

"Well, I don't understand. Why do you need to pick up your car?"

"Marci, please. Could you just come pick me up from the house?"

"All right. I'll be right there," Marci said before she hung up.

Ted wondered how he would explain his impulsive purchase to his daughter, even though she had unknowingly facilitated the idea. He could not see himself staying in a cabin or somebody's rental property as she had suggested. If he had to go away and couldn't stay in a nice hotel, he'd decided to bring the hotel room with him.

His new motorhome boasted a full-size bedroom, a kitchen with a center island, dining table with four chairs, and a living room with an electric fireplace. He knew he would put the two leather recliners to use but didn't think he would ever use the sleep sofa. The bathroom was larger than he expected, and the addition of a clothes washer and dryer sold him on the particular model. Ted loathed the idea of going to a laundromat.

The driver's side consisted of an almost full-length motorized pullout section allowing a large interior living space. The passenger side had a slightly shorter pullout. The driver's cockpit included a monitor for viewing behind the RV and a navigation monitor.

Unfortunately, Ted had been in such a hurry to be done with the purchase, he didn't give the salesman time to show him how all the equipment worked.

He peeked out the living room window to see how it looked in his driveway.

It is quite a machine, Ted thought.

With a shiny black and tan base, decorative white swirls gave it some flair.

"You can do this, Ted," he imagined Carol whispering in his ear.

"*I can do this*," he said.

GOOD MORNING?

SUMMER

Summer had intended to visit the Rock & Roll Hall of Fame in Ohio first, but something changed her mind. Instead, she headed directly to Cayuga Lake in upstate New York. She never made an intentional decision to alter her original plans—she just followed her inner desire to shake things up.

A week after leaving her parents' cottage, Summer sat under the stars next to a roaring campfire with Bruce Springsteen playing through her old transistor radio, a locally produced bottle of wine, and her Jerry Garcia bong by her side. It brought her back to her free-spirited days, long before she needed to care for anyone but herself. And that was how she meant to live the rest of her life.

Heaven, Summer thought. From the time she was a little girl, Summer loved being outdoors. She climbed trees with the boys in her neighborhood, made trails through the woods behind her house, and always exceeded her nighttime curfew when the streetlights turned on. More than once, she used the excuse, "But I didn't see the lights come on."

Because it was so peaceful, she felt it might be difficult to move on from the Cayuga Lake campground she had found. And she had already met some wonderful campers. *Besides*, she reasoned, *the large crowds won't move into the area for at least another month. I'm in no hurry. Maybe I'll stay for a while.*

Summer closed her eyes and refilled her sixty-five-year-old lungs with her favorite blend of cannabis and held her breath.

She heard it first, then opened her eyes and slowly exhaled as the RV turned the corner.

"Jesus, Mother, and Joseph, that's big," she melodically chanted.

The black motorhome slowly made its way down the lane, stopping at every open campsite presumably to check the number etched into the little wooden sign in front of each lot. It became apparent the behemoth would settle in the campsite directly across the lane from hers.

One of the most expensive in the campground, the deluxe premium campsite boasted a fifty-foot deep parking space topped with gravel. Grass covered the rest of the lot with a large firepit on one side and the electrical and sewer hookups on the other. Trees lined the back of the site, and ornamental bushes separated the lots on either side. The campground reserved deluxe premium sites for larger motorhomes and provided ample room for maneuvering. She sipped her wine and watched the massive machine as the driver drove straight into, rather than back into, the lot.

"Well, that's not going to work," Summer chuckled.

From the lane, the motorhome looked parked at a massive angle, the front end on gravel, the rear end on grass. The driver seemed to note the crookedness, backed up cautiously, and tried again. His efforts reduced the awkward positioning but did not completely correct it.

As he tried for a third time, Summer lost her ability to watch in silence. She laughed, a pot-induced cackle that resembled a hyena on helium as it overtook Springsteen's rendition of "Dancing in the Dark."

Apparently satisfied with his last try, the driver, a man wearing a suit and tie, dismounted and walked around the vehicle. In spite of the darkness, Summer could tell he glanced in her direction, which only made her hoot a little louder. The man ascended the stairs to his motorhome, and that was the last Summer saw of him for the evening.

"Wait until he realizes the hookups are on the other side of that thing and he needs to back into the lot," she managed to say out loud through her final round of hysterics.

As her laugh wound down, a twinge of guilt replaced it. *That's just what my father would have done. Laughed.* She shook her head in shame.

"I've got a lot more work to do on myself," she said, then took another hit from her bong.

Early the next morning, Summer sang while she washed herself in her portable outdoor shower. She believed the steaming hot water cleansed her soul as much as her body and thought it the perfect way to start each day. And although she could not carry a tune, singing made her happy. When finished, she wrapped herself in a towel. On the short walk back to her camper, she waved and said "Good morning" to her new neighbor. He seemed embarrassed to see her wearing only a towel, and she chuckled as she entered her trailer.

Shortly thereafter, donning a white shawl and dressed in a colorful caftan, Summer stepped outside and took a deep, cleansing breath. The sun was still low in the sky when she opened the back of her VW bus and stepped on the eight-inch platform she had placed behind the vehicle. The platform, constructed from white PVC pipe, sported a stiff wire mesh top.

Inside the van stood a custom-made wooden box perfectly fitted to the vehicle's width and height. The right half of the box displayed a top to bottom hinged door, and the left side had five drawers. The platform where Summer stood allowed her the extra height that her five-foot, four-inch frame lacked to access the top drawer.

Summer swung open the wooden door of her homemade outdoor kitchen. Hanging from hooks inside were an assortment of pots and pans: some made in Germany, some from France, and some made in the USA. All were top of the line and in pristine condition.

Below the hanging pans lived a three-burner propane stove mounted on a pullout shelf. The stove easily transformed into a grill or griddle by exchanging stovetop accessories. She stored those accessories on the shelf below the pullout. A bracket installed inside the cabinet held a small propane canister to fuel the stove.

Drawers contained items meticulously organized and arranged in order of necessity. The top drawer held items least used, including a juicer, mini meat grinder, and measuring cups. Summer rarely measured ingredients.

The second drawer held mixing bowls and spatulas. The third held whisks, a strainer, a baster, a manual can opener, a cheese grater, and more.

Drawer number four held the most important and necessary items of all, her knives. Each knife had its own slot carved into a wooden insert. Her collection included Wusthof, J.A.Henckel, Shun, and from her early days of cooking, the sentimental favorite, Dexter Russell.

The final drawer, when opened, held a drop-in high-density polypropylene cutting board that could also be used as a countertop. Under the board in separate compartments, she stored grill and griddle cleaning tools, brushes, aprons, and towels.

Soon, the smell of frying bacon made its way across the lane from Summer's stovetop. Then the tantalizing aroma of caramelized onions and garlic followed. Not long after, one could almost taste the savory mushroom omelet as its scent carried in the light breeze.

"Good morning, Summer," a man called from the camper sitting just twenty feet to her right.

"Good morning, Jerry. Good morning, Seamus," she called to Jerry's very friendly Irish Setter. Jerry walked Seamus around the campground every morning, and people shared treats with the dog. Summer had learned that Jerry and his wife, Judy, had been married for eight years and enjoyed their first real vacation away from their home in Pennsylvania.

"Stop by when you've finished your walk, Jerry. I have a homemade peanut butter biscuit for him," Summer said, "and my cinnamon buns might be ready for you by then."

"You're spoiling us, Summer. He's already turning up his nose at the dog biscuits we bought in town," Jerry laughed. "And I'll never be able to eat a store-bought cinnamon bun again."

"Will I see you and Judy for dinner tonight?"

"Wouldn't miss it," Jerry replied as Seamus pulled Jerry in the opposite direction toward his first treat of the day.

STICKY FINGERS

TED

What the heck is that? Ted asked himself as he opened his eyes to the sleep invading screech. Morning sunlight pierced his bedroom window blinds.

At first, he thought a murder of crows had roosted around his RV and cawed.

No, crows don't have a pitch like that.

Then he thought possibly a ferret or a couple of rats had somehow gotten inside, prompting him to jump out of his bed and examine the motorhome thoroughly.

Having ruled out the rodents, he lifted the window shade by his bed and saw nothing, but the sound persisted. Thoroughly invested in finding the source, he put on his bathrobe and slippers and stepped outside.

It was just as cold outside his camper as inside. Crisp, clean air all but smacked him in the face. But the scent reminded him of his newly laundered clothes. The screech returned and redirected his attention. He realized it was not an animal that produced the racket. It came from the lot across from his.

Steam rose from a dark green canvas tent about four feet square and six feet high amid a stand of trees fifteen feet from the tiny old trailer. A water hose protruded from the tent. *An outdoor shower*, he thought. *It's a little cold for that, isn't it?*

The noise stopped. A woman with long wet gray hair and wearing only a beach towel stepped out of the canvas shower.

She spotted him, waved, and yelled, "Good morning."

Unsure what to do, Ted snapped his head to the left and looked away while returning the wave with a dismissive brush of his hand. He immediately stepped back inside his camper.

As he did, he heard the familiar cackle from the previous night. *There's definitely something wrong with that woman*, he thought.

Ted stood at the bathroom sink, topped his toothbrush with minty toothpaste from his shaving kit, and vigorously brushed his teeth. When finished, he turned on the cold water faucet. Nothing came out. He tried the hot water tap. Nothing.

"Darn it," he said as toothpaste bubbles formed in his mouth.

He spit as much of the toothpaste out as possible before remembering he had an open bottle of water in the console by the driver's seat. Having not extended the slideouts on both sides of the camper that created ample interior living space, he had little room to maneuver. He squeezed his way up front and retrieved the water, then returned to the bathroom to rinse his mouth.

He returned to his bedroom to get dressed. Before he left the room, he peered out the window and saw the woman rummaging in her van. He sighed and shook his head. She wore what looked like an old school toga, but colorful.

Hungry, he reached for the box of shredded wheat cereal he had brought. He rummaged through every cabinet and drawer in the kitchen before it struck him that the camper, for all the bells and whistles, did not come with silverware, plates, bowls, or cups.

"You idiot," he mumbled. "You don't have any milk, anyway."

The only food Ted had brought with him was cereal, a half loaf of white bread, peanut butter, and a bag of coffee.

What Ted didn't have was, well, anything else.

Although a highly intelligent and capable lawyer, he had never needed to fend for himself. Carol took care of everything outside his work, and Alex had done most of the cooking and shopping since her passing. Marci hired a cleaning woman to visit his house twice a week. Anything Ted needed had always been where he needed it until then.

I should have asked Alex. He would've set me up.

Annoyed at his lack of attention to details, he used his finger to spoon peanut butter onto a piece of white bread, then licked his finger clean, since he had no water to wash with. He folded the bread in half and placed it on the table.

I've got to figure out how to get water.

He pulled the stack of manuals and paperwork from the large cabinet below the driver's console and dropped them on the table. Morning sunlight didn't provide enough indoor illumination for him to read, so he switched on the overhead light. The light flickered dimly but did not provide enough, either.

The battery must be low. I'm gonna need electricity, too.

Ted brought his manuals, a kitchen chair, and his peanut butter sandwich outside. He was about to open the thick book, but the fragrance of real food forced him to follow the scent. It seemed to come from the crazy woman's camp.

He recognized the aromas: bacon, garlic, mushrooms, onions, and eggs. He longed for one of Alex's French-style omelets, red bliss potato home fries, and fresh squeezed orange juice. He licked his lips then closed his eyes and lifted his chin slightly to allow the fragrance to flow more easily through his nostrils.

The same shrill that had awakened him interrupted his fantasy breakfast. He knew exactly where it came from. The crazy woman sang loudly and poorly. And to make it worse, she belted an Alice Cooper tune. Not exactly a soothing way to start the day, he thought.

Before taking a bite from his dry and pasty peanut butter sandwich, Ted turned his back to the noise and opened his manual.

Used to reading legal documents, Ted found the manual overly complicated and full of disclaimers intended to minimize opportunities for customers to sue the manufacturer. The fact that the company's lawyers felt compelled to warn people not to ingest antifreeze used to winterize their vehicle had Ted shaking his head, although he knew he would recommend the same had they been his clients.

"Hey!" Ted heard someone yell. Without acknowledging it, Ted continued to read.

"Hey, you in the suit!"

Ted looked down at his single-breasted blue suit, then turned his body in the chair to look behind him. She stood at the head of his campsite. She was short and slightly hefty for her height. Her long gray hair had dried, and her outfit betrayed a love for the 1960s. She had a pleasant face and projected an air of confidence.

Ted stood and placed the manual on his chair. He held the half sandwich in his hand.

"Would you like a decent breakfast before you go to work?" she asked as she eyed his peanut butter sandwich. "I've made enough for every one of my past lives."

"Huh? Excuse me?" Ted asked, wondering if he had heard her correctly.

"I made too much food again. And you look like a man who appreciates good food," Summer said.

Ted's eyebrows cinched, and he unconsciously laid his empty hand on his paunchy stomach.

"Oh, I don't mean to imply that you're fat," Summer quickly added. "It's the expensive suit. I just figured if you have good taste in clothing, you probably have good taste in food."

"Well, I . . ." Ted started to say.

"Not that peanut butter doesn't make a great start to your day. It's good protein. But it doesn't hit all those taste buds God gave us."

"God?" Ted asked.

"I always believed that a great day needs to start with a great breakfast," Summer continued with barely a halt. "Especially when you've got a long day of work ahead of you. I always say a beefy breakfast is the base for burying the bullshit."

Ted winced at the stranger's vulgarity.

Summer went on. "I'd be willing to bet most wars have been started on an empty stomach. There's a reason they call it food for the soul, you know. You don't talk much, do you? My name is Summer, Just Summer."

"Ah, Theodore, Theodore Winter," Ted replied.

A high-pitched screech escaped Summer. "Oh, how perfect. Summer and Winter. You know, Teddy, if we ever had children together, we would have had to name them Spring and Fall," Summer cackled.

Ted's mouth dropped open, and his eyes widened in disbelief. "I . . . it's Theodore or Ted. And I don't . . . "

"Oh, relax. I'm just joking with you. Believe me, my eggs dried up long ago," she snickered. "But my omelets haven't, and I do have a lot of food. When do you have to leave for work? I have some cinnamon buns coming out of the oven soon."

"I'm not going to work," Ted said.

"Oh. A funeral, then? Oh, I hope it's not a funeral. That would make for a real bummer of a day," Summer frowned.

"No. I'm not going to a funeral," Ted replied.

"Oh, good," Summer smiled. "Well, what are you all dressed up for?

"These are my clothes," Ted answered, annoyed by the question.

"Your clothes," Summer said with a thump. "Your only clothes?"

"I don't see where it's any business of yours what I . . ."

Summer threw up her hands. "You're right, okay. It's none of my business that you came camping in your thousand-dollar suit," she said with a bit of irony. "So, are you hungry or not?"

"No, thank you," Ted said. And then, remembering his grandmother's nagging about using proper manners, he added, "But thank you for the offer."

"All right, then. It's your loss. I make one hell of an omelet," Summer said, then began to walk back to her camper. She stopped in the middle of the lane that divided their sites, turned, and asked, "Are you planning on using the campsite hookups?"

"Hookups?" he countered.

"Yes. You know, water, electricity, sewer, and cable?"

"Ah, yes. I am."

"Well, you're going to have to turn that rig around," Summer said with a chuckle, then turned to leave. "I've got to go check on my cinnamon buns."

Shortly after, Ted carried his manual and walked around the motorhome, discovering where the pipes, hoses, and outlets hid. As he did, one thing became clear. Summer was right. He would need to turn the motorhome around to connect to the water, electric, and sewer line. That meant he would need to back the forty-foot camper into the campsite.

He'd decided that if he had to move the vehicle, he might as well go to a grocery and department store to stock up on food and equip the kitchen. The campground store sold necessities like soap, laundry detergent, and some canned goods but little else, although you could buy a colorful t-shirt advertising Sunset Pines Campground, his home away from home for the foreseeable future.

He remembered passing a shopping plaza on his way into town, so he climbed into the driver's seat and started the engine. When he glanced at the dashboard, he noticed he was low on gas. Up until then, he had used gas stations on the interstate that were ideal for large trucks and vehicles. He feared he would have trouble maneuvering the camper into a small station in the tiny campground town.

He gingerly backed out of the campsite, a much easier task in daylight. He used the motorhome's rearview camera system to see behind the vehicle. That and large side mirrors made reversing a little less stressful.

He pulled forward, moving at the campground's posted speed of ten miles per hour. *If only I could drive at this pace on the streets,* he thought. He left the campground and headed toward the shopping center. Traffic was heavy, and Ted noticed that most vehicles were turning into the shopping center parking lot. He drove into the lot, scanned the parking area for a large enough space, then headed straight for the exit. He had little confidence in his ability to park the big rig in the space available.

Up the road from the mini mall sat a gas station with wide aisles and a convenience store. Ted felt he could get in and out without much trouble. He silently congratulated himself as he pulled alongside the gas pump, although he noted that he had neglected to park the vehicle perfectly straight. He filled the gas tank and then parked the camper on the far side of the large lot.

Ted entered the convenience store with a mental list of needs, most of which he found. He stacked items by one of the unmanned cash registers and continued to shop. He bought paper goods, food, utensils, and local wine. Then he found a small frying pan and spatula for cooking eggs or grilled cheese sandwiches, two of the few meals he knew how to prepare.

After several rounds through the store, Ted was ready to cash out. He shifted his items to the open cash register. As he paid for his products, he glanced at a display next to the counter of sets of large plastic cups and bowls.

I suppose drinking wine out of a plastic cup is better than a paper cup. And I'll need a bowl for cereal. Oblivious to the set's fanciful design, he added it to the stack.

Ted returned to the campground feeling slightly more confident with his driving skills.

DINNER IS SERVED

SUMMER

Summer watched as the motorhome backed out of the site and drove away. *Too bad*, she thought. *Teddy looked like he needed to unwind. But clearly, he doesn't know how.*

With her morning cleanup finished, Summer placed a blanket on the ground and sat resembling a pretzel, her knees bent and legs crossed in front of her. She rested her hands, palms up, on her knees with each index finger touching its respective thumb.

She closed her eyes and began to chant quietly at first, then rose in pitch as time passed. So deep in her meditation, Summer would not have budged had a herd of elephants stormed the campground. The sound of the large motorhome rounding the bend, however, prompted her to open one eye.

Well, this is a surprise, she thought, certain that her neighbor had abandoned the idea of camping. She closed her eye and concluded her meditation with her personal mantra, the one she had written to soothe her soul as a young woman trying to find her place in the world. *I am who I am. I am who I'm going to be. I'm going to be who I am.*

When she opened her eyes, she saw that Ted planned to back his massive camper into the site. Not only did Summer watch with great anticipation, but she also concentrated on channeling vibes of confidence to him.

He pulled past the site and cut his wheels. Slowly, he backed up. Summer eyed him in the driver's seat. His head snapped back and forth as if watching a ping pong match as he alternated his attention between the two side mirrors.

The firepit, she panicked. *Does he see the firepit?*

She was about to jump up and scream when the motorhome lurched backward and crashed into the concrete cinderblocks of the pit. Summer glanced back at Ted and saw him animatedly chastising himself. She decided to turn away before he noticed her observing, but she was too late. Ted's eyes locked onto hers, and they seemed to convey culpability.

Summer turned her back to the action and walked toward the back of her van. She heard him rev the motorhome engine. With peripheral vision, she saw Ted pull forward, then back the vehicle into a slightly crooked position. Then, masking her scrutiny by standing behind the open back door of her van, she watched him step out of the driver's seat, assess the angle of his parking, and get back into the RV.

Huh. A perfectionist. Why doesn't that surprise me?

It took two more adjustments before Ted seemed satisfied with the positioning, and Summer could stop pretending not to watch. She made a point to slam her vehicle's back door shut as if to announce her imaginary task had concluded.

"Don't worry, Teddy. It happens all the time," Summer yelled to Ted as he examined the back of his motorhome.

She received a simple wave in return. Not a happy, nice-to-see-you-wave but one reserved to shoo away a fly.

The afternoon hours passed quickly as Summer engaged in her favorite pastime—cooking. Since early childhood, she had found comfort in food—first in eating, later in preparation. Her fondest memories were of baking sweets with her mother. Growing up, due to her father's preference, main meals consisted of meat and potatoes. But desserts were highly encouraged, and Delores used the opportunity to express her creativity. Summer cherished that time with her. Occasionally, her father complimented Delores on her cakes and pies. Those would be the only times Summer recalled hearing any kind words from her father.

Summer had her hands deep into her honey biscuit dough. As nights still held a chill, Summer tended toward stews and casseroles for the evening meal. Flaky biscuits complemented her large batch of merlot-infused beef stew, which sat simmering on her stove.

She used her folding table covered with a silicone baking mat to roll the biscuit dough to one-half inch thick. Taking her stemmed wine glass, Summer pressed the open top into the dough to cut the biscuits into uniformly sized rounds. When finished, she brushed the tops of the biscuits with honey butter, sprinkled them with a scant amount of nutmeg, and placed them in her oven. Twelve minutes later, they sat cooling on a wire rack.

"It's time," Summer said. She reached for her mallet and headed outside.

TED

His stomach upset, Ted inspected the damage to the back end of the RV. As he hadn't been moving too fast, he only found minor scratches on the bumper. He concluded that he could buff the scratches out. Still, his ineptness in maneuvering his rig agitated him and that his lack of skill had been witnessed annoyed him. He spent the remainder of the day restacking his firepit, reading his manual, and connecting to the campground amenities.

Ted rolled up his sleeves and adjusted the stabilizer feet until the camper was perfectly level. Then he extended the large slideout by simply pushing a switch. He was pleased at the amount of room it created. He let out the second slider and smiled. *This is nice*, he thought. Next, he pushed another switch, and the outdoor awning rolled out, running from the front door of the camper to the rear pullout section to provide him shade from the sun and protection from any rain that might occur.

He found the hose in a compartment on the outside of the camper and hooked up the water. Then he slid the three-pronged, fifty-amp electrical plug into the outlet the campground provided. He turned the propane gas on for heat and set the hot water heater to use electricity. Because he didn't look forward to it, he saved the sewer connection for last.

Once he removed the accordion-style sewer hose from its storage and attached it to the camper, he connected it to the site's septic tank hookup. Ted was pleasantly surprised he didn't detect more of an odor.

After a rough start to the day, he felt he had exonerated himself. But what should have taken less than an hour had taken him all day to accomplish. He would have saved a lot of time if he had only allowed the RV salesperson to complete his pitch and tell him about hookups. But when he stepped back inside, he felt at home.

Ted poured Pinot Noir into his new plastic cup and sat in front of the electric fireplace. It was only then that he noticed frolicking unicorns decorating his blue cup. He chuckled, then took a sip. *Okay. Tomorrow I'll figure out the cable TV and internet*, Ted thought, feeling satisfied.

It was nearly six o'clock when he heard a loud sound and glanced out the front window of his RV.

"What in the world?" he murmured.

He set his empty wine cup on the kitchen island, moved to the driver's console, and watched, dumbfounded, as Summer swung a long-handled mallet against what looked like a large drum set cymbal suspended from a tree branch. He hadn't noticed it before, as his vantage point came from its side. He could see only the sliver of its edge.

The vibrating sound could be attributed to just one instrument.

"Is that a . . . a gong?"

Moments later, he watched campers step out of their motorhomes and trailers, carrying plates and bowls. They formed a line across the lane in front of Summer's campsite.

Filling his cup with wine and taking it with him, Ted went outside to see what was going on. He approached the last two people in line, an elderly gentleman with his wife.

"Excuse me," he said. "What's the line for?"

The man replied, "It's beef stew and biscuits tonight."

"Oh," Ted said as if that was all the explanation he needed.

He stood to the side and watched Summer greet each person by name as she dished out a generous portion of stew and what he presumed to be a biscuit wrapped in a napkin. Some people lingered for a short conversation, while others just smiled and walked away with their meal.

He saw some of the diners put money into a coffee can sitting on the table. As he watched, the smell of stew permeated his senses. It made his mouth water.

Summer spotted him and brightened her smile, "It's nice to see you at least took your suit jacket off. Are you hungry, Teddy?"

He winced at the use of the nickname.

"It's Ted. No, thank you. I already have dinner planned. I confess I got curious when I heard the gong," he said.

"Yeah, it's a gas, isn't it?" Summer said as she continued to serve.

"Do you do this often?"

"Most every night. I post the evening meal on the bulletin board in front of the store."

"Ah," was all Ted could think of saying. "Well, goodnight."

"Goodnight, Teddy."

Ted closed his eyes, counted to ten, and walked away to keep himself from getting annoyed at Summer's persistent use of the nickname.

It didn't work.

⌒⌒

The addition of a working heater allowed Ted to sleep soundly that night. He woke to the sun rising and birds singing. He lingered in bed, something he never did at home. Ted couldn't remember ever hearing birds chirp in the morning. He wondered if he couldn't hear them from his bedroom at home or if he just didn't notice them. He allowed himself a good morning stretch before hopping out of bed and into a hot shower. Having forgotten to buy shampoo, he used the bar soap to wash his salt and pepper hair, *the salt far outnumbering the pepper these days*, he thought.

He opted not to don a suit jacket that morning, instead dressing in black suit pants and a starched white shirt fresh from the dry cleaners.

At that point, his serene morning ceased.

Something resembling singing reached from across the lane to assault his ears. This time, it took the form of the Led Zeppelin song "Stairway to Heaven."

Ted looked out his front window and saw steam rising from the canvas tent. His instincts told him to look away, but it was too late. Summer emerged only partially covered by her beach towel, her backside opting for the air dry method.

Feeling like a voyeur, Ted quickly turned away even though Summer did not seem to worry if anyone saw her. He found it disconcerting that a person could be so audacious.

Grateful that Led Zeppelin no longer rambled, Ted tuned his radio to a classical music station and removed eggs and bread from his refrigerator. Not having a toaster, he decided to grill the white bread in the frying pan. He slathered butter on the bread, placed it in the pan, and fried it over high heat until smoke began to rise. The unmistakable smell of burning bread filled the camper. He removed it, singed on the edges and white and soggy in the middle and placed it on the counter beside the stove.

Then he cracked two eggs into the hot frying pan. The yolks broke on impact, and the whites immediately attached themselves to the bottom of the pan. With his spatula, he tried to scrape the eggs off, managing to flip portions of them into the remnants of burned bread crumbs.

As he tried to remove the eggs, the metal spatula scratched the bottom of his convenience store non-stick frying pan. The bulk of his breakfast flew out of the pan and onto the soggy toast sitting on the counter. The remainder of the eggs refused to budge.

There was a knock at his door.

Ted placed the pan back on the stove and opened the door.

"Good morning, Teddy. I brought you some cinnamon buns," Summer said as she climbed the stairs into his camper. "Oh, what's burning?" She scanned the kitchen to make sure there was no fire.

"Nothing. Just some toast," Ted replied. "I really apprec— . . ."

"This is pitiful," Summer interrupted, staring at Ted's eggs and bread.

She placed the perfectly moist and tantalizingly decorated cinnamon buns on Ted's table, then began to clean the egg from the counter, scraping it with her hands.

"You don't need to . . ."

"Take it easy. I'm going to make you breakfast. Just sit back and relax."

"But I . . ."

"You don't drink coffee?" she asked.

"Yes, I . . ."

"Well, where is it?" Summer searched.

"I don't have a coffee pot," Ted replied.

Summer finished cleaning the counter, threw away the burned white bread, and set the frying pan to soak in the sink. "I'll be right back," she said.

"You don't have . . ."

She left before Ted could finish the sentence and returned moments later carrying a full pot of coffee, a frying pan, and a rubber spatula.

"Where are your coffee cups?" she asked.

"Ah, I don't have any," Ted replied.

Summer looked at Ted and shook her head. "You haven't put much thought into this camping thing, have you."

"I . . . "

"Never mind." She reached for the blue plastic cup sitting upside down on a paper towel by the sink. She studied the unicorns. "Cute," she chuckled. "I took you for more of a Smurf kind of guy."

Not understanding the reference, Ted crinkled his brow.

Summer poured coffee into the plastic cup. "Milk?"

"No, I really don't need . . . "

"Sugar?"

"No," Ted said sharply.

"Here. Start with a cinnamon bun. Breakfast will be ready in a jiff," Summer said as she placed his coffee on the table and pushed the plate of cinnamon buns in front of him. She folded a piece of paper towel and placed it beside the dish.

With the white bread still sitting on the counter, Summer turned the gas stove on low and placed a piece of it directly on top of the burner. She kept moving the bread until it was golden brown on one side, then turned it over and did the same. She made a second piece of toast while she heated butter in her frying pan on another burner. She dropped two eggs in the pan. Part way through cooking, she picked up the frying pan and, with a quick flip of her wrist and a slight jerking motion, the eggs gently jumped from the pan, turned over, and landed softly back in the pan without breaking the yolks.

"How did you do that?" Ted asked.

"The equipment makes all the difference, Teddy."

"It's Ted. Look, I appreciate all this, but . . ."

"You don't look like a Ted. Ted is too stuffy. You look more like a Teddy to me." Summer placed the buttered toast and over easy eggs in front of him.

"You really didn't . . ."

"I know. You don't need any help. But sometimes people just want to help, and it's a nice gesture to let them," Summer smiled. "Enjoy your breakfast. I'll pick up the coffee pot later," she said. And suddenly, she was gone, taking her frying pan and spatula with her.

Ted sat with his mouth agape. *What the hell just happened?* He looked down at his paper plate of toast and eggs and noticed how expertly cooked they were. The toast was browned, just as he liked it, and the eggs waited for his fork to sink into bright orange runny yolk. But it was aromatic cinnamon mixed with a hint of vanilla in the buns that demanded his attention. He lifted glazed pastry topped with crushed walnuts and sunk his teeth into moist, buttery dough . . . perfection. He made quick work of the first bun and considered diving into the second but heard his daughter's voice in his head—*I'm afraid that you don't want to put the effort in.*

He did, however, polish off the toast and eggs with a second cup of excellent coffee before placing his hand on his full stomach and belching.

"Maybe a little help now and then wouldn't be such a bad thing," he muttered.

He washed his dishes and wiped down the stove and countertop. He poured the remaining coffee into the plastic bowl, covered it, and placed it in the refrigerator. Then he sat down to make a list.

Summer had been correct, Ted conceded. He hadn't put much thought into "this camping thing." He never had to be the one to stock an empty refrigerator or equip a kitchen, bathroom, bedroom, or living room. With pen in hand, he mentally scanned the drawers and cabinets of his home back in Newton going room by room, jotting down items such as a toaster, trash bucket, and laundry basket. He determined that on his next foray out in the motorhome, he would find a way to park in the department store parking lot.

He decided to return the cleaned coffee pot himself rather than wait for Summer to pick it up, but when he stepped outside and glanced over to her site, he found her sitting on the ground with her hands resting on her knees. She mumbled as she meditated. He'd made the mistake of once interrupting Marci while meditating. After her outburst, he never made it again. Ted remembered thinking that Marci must have been in desperate need of meditation to react so vehemently.

Instead of returning the coffee pot, Ted decided to dig into the owner's manual again and learn how to set up the camper's television and cable connections. Never particularly good with electronics, he took several attempts to match plugs to outlets, scolding himself with each misstep, but he eventually succeeded and allowed himself a metaphorical pat on the back. He was about to turn on a news program when his cell phone rang. It was Marci.

"Hi, Dad. How are things?" Marci asked, sounding annoyed.

"Fine, Marci. And with you?" he asked.

"Come on, Dad. Don't play coy with me. You left without a word. Imagine my surprise when I went by the house and didn't find your hotel on wheels in your driveway. Where are you?" she asked.

"You're the one who insisted I get away, Marci."

"Yes, but I didn't want you to disappear without a trace. So, where are you?"

"I'm in New York."

"That's a pretty big state, Dad. Could you narrow it down for me a bit?"

"Why?" Ted asked, worried that she might hop in her car and join him.

"Why? Because you're my father who just had his second heart attack and I don't think it's a good idea for you to go incommunicado at this point. I mean, I'm glad you're getting away, but I thought we would have had more of a discussion about where and how far you would go."

Ted heard a knock on his door. Before he had a chance, Summer opened the door and stepped inside.

"You do realize that you are the child and I am the parent, right?" Ted said, rolling his eyes after realizing that Summer stood in his trailer.

"Don't let me bother you. I just came for the coffee pot," Summer said.

"Dad," Marci yelled into the phone, "who's that? Where are you?"

"Look, Marci, we'll talk about this later. I'll call you tonight," Ted said before he hung up the phone.

"Trouble with the family?" Summer asked.

"You can't just barge into people's homes . . . or trailers any time you want," Ted barked.

"I could see you were busy. I didn't want to interrupt you," Summer replied.

"You could see I was busy?"

"Yes. If you don't want people looking into your motorhome, you should lower the shade by your windshield. Otherwise, it's like a big television screen."

"What?"

"Anyway, I saw you on the phone and didn't want to disturb you. But I need my coffee pot so I can make strong coffee to put into my espresso cannoli tonight. Shall I expect you for dinner?"

"What? No."

Summer reached for the coffee pot then turned to leave.

"Don't worry, Teddy. I'm sure Marci will forgive you for hanging up on her," Summer smiled before she exited.

Ted threw his hands in the air and let out a bellowed grunt. "Arghhh. One, two, three, four, five, six, seven, eight, nine, ten." Ted breathed in deeply. "It's going to take a lot more counting than that to deal with this birdbrain," he said aloud.

Ted pulled the manual for the motorhome from the drawer, learned how to close the shade at the front of his trailer, and proceeded to do so. Then he locked the camper door.

BEE HAPPY

TED

After his frustrating morning, Ted enjoyed a quiet day. He attributed his tranquility to realizing that Summer had been away all day.

He took a walk around the campground, occasionally stopping to speak with other campers. He found himself examining the setups at each site. Ted was captivated by Ilene and Ned Stromberg, a retired couple who owned a motorhome similar in size to his. They told him they had sold their house in Michigan two years before and had been living on the road ever since.

"We live like nomads," Ilene told Ted. "We spend our winters in the South and move to the North during the warmer months."

A long strand of lights hung from their awning, and the portable outdoor furniture wouldn't have looked out of place on Ted's Newton patio back home. Firewood was piled near the back edge of their site protected from rain by a ten-foot by ten-foot canopy.

Some campers, like novices Jerry and Judy, used basic folding tables and chairs with electric or kerosene lanterns while others took the added step of decorating their sites with silk flowers, wind chimes, and whirligigs. But everyone had something, except for Ted. If he wished to sit outside, he needed to drag out the wooden kitchen chair. And he would sit in the dark except for the minimal lighting built into the outdoor awning and not providing nearly enough light to read. He also didn't have any firewood.

"It would be nice to sit by a real fire tonight," Ted murmured as he walked toward the campground store.

He found that the store stocked more than he originally had noticed. He recognized the woman behind the counter as the campground owner but could not remember her name.

When he asked if he could have firewood delivered to his site, she replied, "Absolutely. We can deliver whatever you need."

Ted wandered through the small store and found a collapsible canvas chair in a bag, a small fold-up camp table, lighter fluid, matches, and a battery-operated lantern. While stacking the items in a pile, he glanced at the rack of clothing. He spotted a navy blue sweatshirt in his size and embroidered with *Sunset Pines at Cayuga Lake, NY*. He shrugged his shoulders and tossed it on the pile.

"Could you deliver this to site Number 53, please, with five bundles of firewood?" he asked.

"You bet. I'll have my son deliver it as soon as he gets home from school," the woman replied.

Ted paid for his purchases and thanked her. Outside, he scanned the bulletin board. Among flyers announcing activities taking place in town for the month of May, a bright yellow piece of paper decorated with hand-drawn flowers and honeybees was tacked to the board. The paper was titled "Tonight's Dinner-May 20." The menu included homemade lasagna, dinner roll, and espresso cannoli. At the bottom of the page was a smiley face surrounded with hearts.

This must be how she makes a living, Ted thought.

After a leisurely stroll back to his campsite, he inspected the firepit. A layer of stone covered the bottom, and remnants of previous fires were minimal. When he glanced up, he noticed a large panel on the outside of his camper and realized he had never inspected what was beneath it.

When he unlocked the panel, it arced out and up to create a five-foot wide roof cover. When flipped, a switch on the inside wall illuminated an outdoor kitchen. A small refrigerator sat on a countertop to eliminate any need to go inside the camper for cold food and beverages. A storage drawer sat under the refrigerator. To the right of the drawer was a built-in, pullout gas stove with accessories to convert the cooktop into a grill or griddle. Ted found accessories stored in the drawer. He found an outdoor television mounted above the counter with recessed speakers on either side.

"Wow," Ted said. "This is great."

He pictured himself cooking a burger, watching a football game, and drinking a beer while relaxing in his canvas chair by a roaring fire.

"Carol would have loved this," he whispered as sadness overtook him.

He stood still and silent. He wondered if he and Carol would have ever entertained the idea of a nomad life. For several moments, he pictured what that life might have looked like for the two of them. Then he switched off the light and closed the panel.

As he stepped inside his motorhome, all he could think was how he used to have everything he ever wanted: a wonderful wife, a child he adored, and a job he loved. Two out of those three were gone.

His thoughts brought him to a time when his life seemed perfect. He remembered rushing home to Carol and Marci after a gratifying day at work. He would tell Carol about his day, and she would regale him with sweet and funny stories about her students. The glow on her face as she spoke about her work always captured his heart. *It's interesting*, he thought, *how after five years, my memories usually take me to the wonderful, ordinary times we shared instead of fixating on her last months before cancer took her away from me.* His heart both ached and loved to go back to those happy, ordinary days.

He sat in his recliner and dialed a number from his cell phone.

"Marci, it's Dad," he said when she answered.

"Dad, I'm sorry I was such a . . . well, you know. I'm sorry about this morning. I overreacted," Marci said.

"No, honey, you were right. I should have told you where I was going, but to be honest, I really didn't know. I had an idea I might go to Ohio to see the Pro Football Hall of Fame, but when I got here, it seemed like a good place to stop for a time."

"Where, exactly, are you?" Marci asked.

"I'm in a campground by Cayuga Lake in New York. It's wine country here," Ted chuckled.

"It's a beautiful area. Frank and I spent time at Seneca Lake before we had the boys," Marci said with a smidge of nostalgia.

"You should come visit and stay the weekend. This thing sleeps six people. It really is big," Ted laughed.

"I would love that, but we have plans for this weekend. Maybe next weekend if you are still there. Casey and Frankie would love it. I'll talk to Frank. Do you like the motorhome?"

"I'm still learning about everything, but yes, I think I do."

"And the campground is nice?" Marci asked.

"It is. It's peaceful, except for the crazy lady across the way from me. She's a bit of a ditz."

"Dad! That's not like you. I've never heard you say a questionable word about anyone," Marci said with a hint of a smile behind her words.

"She owns a gong, Marci. You would understand if you saw her," Ted said.

Marci chuckled. "I hope I get the opportunity. I need to pick the boys up from school now. Thanks for calling, Dad. I love you."

"I love you, too, pumpkin. We'll talk again soon," Ted said.

Ted felt a calmness roll over him. It lasted until about four-thirty when he saw the VW bus pull into the site across the lane. Instinctively, his nerves jumped.

BEE-ING

SUMMER

Summer looked forward to her late morning adventure. And she had a perfect spring day for it. Including taking a tour of one of her favorite wineries, she had attained a coveted spot in the vineyards *Bee Happy* interactive educational session.

Johnson Family Orchards produced wines under various labels, the most popular the appropriately named Avant-Garde. Known for pairing unusual flavors, the winery had become a favorite tourist attraction in the Finger Lakes region.

Once a year on World Bee Day, the Johnsons opened their beekeeping activities to six lucky lottery winners. Summer had entered the contest online while sitting in the kitchen of her parents' little white cottage. The winners of the contest could purchase a coveted opportunity for a small, private tour of the facility including a tutorial on the business of beekeeping and a private wine tasting. She got the call three months earlier. Winning the raffle gave her the extra push she needed to put things in order. Without the deadline, she might have procrastinated and not moved out of her parents' house, a change she needed to make to get on with her life. Once notified, Summer knew her trip to Cayuga Lake was meant to be.

She arrived at the vineyard thirty minutes early where a delightful young woman named Andi escorted her. By the time they wove through the back rooms of the main building, Summer had learned that Andi was seventeen years old, the granddaughter of the current owners, and learning the business from the ground up, just the way her grandfather had. So far, Andi most liked working in the tasting room, where she met people from around the world.

Apologizing for her need to get back to work, Andi left Summer in a small room near the back of the building. She pointed to a pot of honey tea sitting on a warmer and said, "Please, help yourself."

The room resembled a library you might see in an expensive hotel or mansion, only smaller. Paisley-covered high-backed chairs sat among Shaker-style wooden ones with side tables scattered about.

Summer helped herself to a cup of tea and scanned the bookshelves. She found volumes on beekeeping, winemaking, cheese-making, and cookbooks. She also found classics such as *A Tale of Two Cities, The Great Gatsby*, and *Harry Potter*.

Tempted to reach for *Harry Potter*, Summer chose instead *"Handbook for the Beginning Beekeeper."* She sat in one of the high-backed chairs and, thinking how much her mother would have loved the sweet brew, placed her scrumptious tea on a side table. Fingering the pages of the well-worn book, she stopped on a chapter titled "Robber Bees." Intrigued, she began to read.

Shortly thereafter, a man and woman entered the room. She estimated them to be only slightly younger than herself.

"Hello." Summer put the book down and greeted them as they entered.

"Hello," the woman said with a British accent. "Are you here for the beekeeping tutorial as well?"

"Yes, I am," Summer replied, "I am excited to be here. My name is Summer," she replied.

"This is my husband, Howard, and I am June. It's lovely to meet you," June said as Howard nodded to Summer.

"Did you come here from England, or do you live in the States?" Summer asked.

"We are here on holiday," June replied. "We live in Liverpool. When we won the contest, we knew we had to come. How thrilling. Harold is a beekeeper."

With a thick British accent, Harold spoke, "Well, no, not really. I'm just learning, aren't I? But I have begun my own hive. Langstroth, you see. Quite a common breed."

Next through the door came a young man with dark skin, high cheekbones, and engaging green eyes. Clearly of American Indian heritage, Joseph hailed from South Dakota and attended Cornell University in Ithaca, New York. He majored in entomology, the study of insects and their relationship to the environment. As they spoke, Summer learned of Joseph's goal to protect the recently threatened honeybee.

The last couple to join the group announced they were on their honeymoon. Blake and Cassie Norwood lived in Pennsylvania and dreamed of someday owning their own vineyard. They were twenty-two and twenty one years old, respectively.

Precisely at noon, Roger Johnson entered. A brusque looking man, his demeanor was anything but. He stood tall with a hefty frame and waistline that looked as if it could ingest a healthy amount of food. A white beard and mustache graced his seventy-five-year-old face, and his hands were large and leathery.

"Good day, everyone. My name is Roger, and I am pleased to have you as our guests. Today is World Bee Day. In 2017, the country of Slovenia proposed the idea for this day, and the United Nations member states approved. Since then, we at Johnson Family Orchards have also been doing our small part in educating people on the importance of protecting bees.

"If bees become extinct," he continued, "it's likely the human race will follow. Today is only one way we try to help. All the money you paid to be here today, along with other fundraising activities, goes toward those three main goals, so I want to thank you all for your generous donation. Shall we begin?"

Roger led the group outside to an area seen by the public only through a window in the wine tasting room. The prize tour brought the winners to the field profuse with goldenrod, asters, dandelions, and several other native plant varieties along with a beautiful view of Cayuga Lake beyond. Amid the fragrant field sat a plethora of stacked wooden boxes, each roughly ten inches in height with stacks ranging from four to seven bins high.

"Welcome to the Johnson Family apiary," Roger began. "Those wooden stacks you see are our hives. If you look closely, you can see the bees from here even though we are still a good twenty yards from the first hive."

The guests concentrated their eyes on the field.

"Ahhh, I see them," Cassie screeched excitedly. "Will we be getting closer to them?"

"Yes," Roger replied. "But first, we are going to sit here, and I'm going to tell you why bees are instrumental in winemaking, even though the grapevines do not need bees to pollinate them like most plants do."

Cassie seemed disappointed and took a seat on one of three benches laid out before them.

"Let's talk about sex," Roger said.

Cassie raised her eyebrows and sat up straight, as did the others.

"I see I have your attention," Roger snickered. "Possessing the reproductive characteristics of both male and female, grapevines self-pollinate. They do not rely on bees or any other insect to fertilize them. So, why do we need bees, you might ask?"

Summer nodded her head, confirming that would have been the first question that came from her lips.

"Because of the soil, they grow in. Look around the field and tell me what you see," Roger said.

"Flowers," Cassie spurted while raising her hand as if in school.

"Goldenrod, dandelion, asters, and clover," Joseph added.

"Very good," Roger said as he focused his gaze on Howard and June.

"Um, you've got some maple and apple trees," Howard said.

"That's right. Trees factor into this, too. Very good," Roger agreed.

"And you?" Roger looked at Summer. "What do you see out there?"

Summer thought for just a moment, then replied, "I see the cycle of life."

Roger smiled and said, "I couldn't have said it better myself."

For the next hour and a half, they learned about how bees fortify the soil and how the flavors of honey change from season to season as the cover growth around them changes. Joseph asked about robber bees, while Howard wanted to delve into the specifics of extracting the honey from hives.

They donned protective equipment before approaching the hives—large gloves and a head covering with a built-in hat draped with fine see-through mesh attached to a smock that safeguarded their upper body from potential bee stings. Summer handed June her cell phone to take her picture as she stood by a hive with bees swarming around her.

Roger's presentation finished, he led the group to a table in the tasting room where Andi took over. She treated them to five samplings of different varieties of wine, explaining in great detail the flavors and textures while they enjoyed delectable canapés made with Johnson Family honey and wines.

Summer could not have enjoyed herself more. After saying goodbye and wishing her new friends well, Summer took a moment to sit on a bench outside the winery tasting room and gazed toward the lake. She thought about Blake and Cassie and how their lives were just beginning. And Joseph, who possessed a noble cause, had a lifetime ahead of him and the ability to do his part to save the world.

Then she smiled as she thought of Howard and June. She saw in them herself and Arnold. She wondered how different the previous fifteen years would have been if Arnold were still alive.

Summer clutched the bag with her complimentary bottle of wine and the few souvenirs, including honey, she had purchased from the gift shop, and headed to her van.

"Goodbye, bees. Thank you for what you do. I will send you healthy vibes," Summer said as she turned the key.

When she returned to the campground, Summer didn't waste any time. She unpacked her day's bounty and went straight to work on dinner. She had already prepared most of the lasagna. All that was left was to put it together and pop it in to bake. She filled two of the largest rectangle casserole dishes she could fit in her Shasta's custom-fit oven.

With two hours left before she planned to wallop the gong, Summer began work on her espresso cannoli filling. Chocolate shells she had prepared before leaving for the winery sat on a parchment-lined sheet pan waiting for their delectable center. She used a rubber spatula to mix ricotta cheese, confectioner's sugar, and crushed dark chocolate bits. Then she added pure vanilla and the strong espresso she brewed after getting her pot back from Ted.

Dipping her finger into the bowl, she lifted a mound of coffee ecstasy into her mouth. She closed her eyes and moaned as if her life's desire had just been fulfilled. Summer spooned the mixture into her piping bag and jam-packed the cannoli shells, first from one end, then the other. She melted the excess dark chocolate and lightly drizzled it over the shells, then dusted them with confectioner's sugar.

She was ready for dinner with time to spare. Summer opened her new bottle of wine, then went outside and sat down for the first time since she got back. That's when she noticed Ted's campsite. A canvas camp chair sat next to the firepit aside a small table with firewood piled on the backside of the pit.

Why, Teddy. You surprise me, Summer smiled to herself. *Maybe you are finally beginning to lighten up.*

Judging by his impeccable dressing habit, she hadn't thought him the type to enjoy sitting by a fire. *You don't find too many expensive suits hanging out by the willowing smoke and flying embers,* she thought. *Just another example of why I should not assume I know a person until I know a person,* Summer scolded herself.

A chuckle escaped when she saw Ted had closed the shade at the front of his camper, but the laugh didn't last long. The closed shade reminded her of her father. In his later days, when the effects of Alzheimer's turned him to fear, she struggled to keep him from hiding behind drapes and bed sheets. She sometimes found him in the hall closet, shielding himself with the hanging coats. A tiny tear formed in the corner of her eye.

Although she and her father had had a strained relationship, she loved him. She just hadn't liked him very much. He had always been judgmental, irritable, rude, and arrogant. Summer hated the way he had treated her mother as if she were a worker bee, only there to serve him. But in her heart, she knew their relationship served a purpose, and she was grateful for that.

Summer lifted her wine glass to the sky and said, "Cheers, Dad! I hope you are buzzing around the heavens like a bee in a field of wildflowers." She took a sip of the Pinot Noir and smiled. Then, just to take the edge off, she reached for her cannabis pipe and lighter.

She sounded the gong at exactly 5:55, and the line began to form. Summer knew the night's menu would be popular. *After all, who doesn't like espresso cannoli?* she thought. In fact, she came perilously close to running out of food before she filled the last person's plate at 6:45.

Feeling gratified and only a little weary, Summer began to pack up what few leftovers remained when an idea struck her. Onto one of her dinner plates she placed the last of the lasagna, enough to feed three people, and covered it with foil wrap. She then put two cannoli and three dinner rolls on a paper plate, covered it, and with both hands full, walked across the street to Ted's door.

Unable to knock, she called out, "Teddy, open the door!"

She heard movement in the camper, but the door remained closed.

"Teddy!" she screamed louder. "Open up before I drop this and you end up with an Italian smorgasbord on your doorstep."

The door slowly opened, and Ted peeked out.

"What is it?" he asked.

"Hurry up and grab one of these plates," Summer said in a panic.

"But I don't . . ."

"Just take the goddam plate. I'm about to lose it."

"All right," Ted said, reaching down to take the plastic dish.

Summer took hold of the paper plate with both hands and winced.

Ted stood in the doorway with the lasagna in his hands.

"Well, go put it down and take this one," Summer huffed, shaking her head as if trying to reason with a two-year-old.

"But I don't want . . ."

Summer let out a sigh and placed the cannoli and dinner rolls on Ted's doorstep. She grimaced as she wrung her hands together.

Ted noticed. "Are you okay?"

"Goddam arthritis," she muttered. "Sometimes my hands just cramp up on me without warning." Then, Summer looked at Ted holding the plate and said, "Well, are you just going to stand there?"

By then, the smell of fresh tomatoes, basil, and oregano had taken residence in Ted's nostrils. He found himself breathing in deeply to satisfy his olfactory senses.

"Look, I don't know what you want, but I'm not interested in . . . "

"What I want?" Summer interrupted. "What do you think I want?"

"I don't know. You keep snooping around here and . . . "

"Snooping?" Summer's eyes compressed, and she pursed her lips. "I had some leftover food, and I was trying to be neighborly. But don't worry." She turned on her heels. "I won't bother you again," she went on as she stormed away, leaving the cannoli and dinner rolls on Ted's doorstep.

"Wait, I didn't mean to . . . " Ted's voice trailed off.

With a wave of her hand, Summer continued to walk away, and her eyes welled with tears.

While packing up the food, she had told herself that she wanted to do something nice to make up for walking in on Ted's telephone conversation with his daughter that morning. But as she marched away from his door, she conceded that wasn't the real reason she brought him the leftovers. Summer did not believe in coincidence or chance. *Teddy and I were put here together for a reason*, she had thought. She believed that maybe she was meant to help Ted. *Maybe I'm here to teach him how to relax and enjoy life.*

But things didn't go as planned, and instead, he hurt her feelings. But more than hurt feelings, it was Ted's unfortunate choice of words that hit her hard.

Memories brought her back to when her father dismissed her as a snoop and a bother. She would run to her mother, crying, and her mother would advise, "Your father's inability to connect with people is his luggage to carry, not yours. Remember, you pack your own bags. Discard the things that do not serve you." Years passed before Summer understood what her mother tried then to convey. Delores had packed her own bag, and it included Summer's father. It was entirely up to Summer to decide the contents that would serve her own life. And at that moment, Ted was not making the cut.

She abruptly stopped walking as she reached the boundary of her campsite.

"No," she said. "I will not let someone else impose their negativity on me. I am who I am. I am who I'm going to be, and I'm going to be who I am," she murmured.

She stood tall, wiped the tears from her eyes, and continued to her trailer.

TOO MANY ASSUMPTIONS

TED

Ted placed the lasagna on the table and retrieved the paper plate from his doorstep. A delightful smell soon engulfed the large space, overpowering the odor of new leather furniture.

He stood motionless over the table and peered at the two plates.

"You are such an idiot, Ted," he uttered.

He felt terrible. *Yes, I got annoyed with Summer, and she does have boundary issues,* he thought, *but that's no reason to be dismissive of her feelings.*

And besides, if the lasagna was as good as her cinnamon rolls, he looked forward to digging in.

But he couldn't. Guilt prevented him from lifting the aluminum foil to take a peek at the meal that had his tastebuds tingling.

Ted sighed. Understanding that he should apologize, he chose a bottle of wine from his cabinet. Thinking it might be chilly, he donned his new sweatshirt and headed across the lane.

Summer, usually outside her camper, was nowhere to be seen. He noticed movement inside. Through daisy-spattered curtains, Ted could see she stood at the sink drying her dishes.

He knocked on her door.

Without first asking who was there, Summer, wearing an apron, swung her door open.

"Oh, it's you!" she spat.

Ted stood with his mouth open, prepared to speak, but could only manage an inaudible sound.

"What?" Summer hissed. "Am I washing my dishes too loud for you?"

"I'm sorry," Ted blurted with more volume than he intended. Then, in a more sedate tone, he repeated, "I'm sorry."

Summer wiped her hands with the dish towel, folded it, and placed it on the counter behind her.

"Okay, you're sorry. I accept your apology. Goodnight," she said as she reached for her door to close it.

Ted used his arm to stop the door from closing. "Wait. I mean it," he said. "I really am sorry. I'm just not used to this."

"Used to what?" Summer asked.

Ted paused, then responded, "Meeting people."

Summer shoved her hands into her apron pockets. "Oh, come on, Teddy. You don't get to be your age without meeting a few people."

"Socially, I mean. I meet new people every day at work, and it's easy. But my wife was always the one who handled social situations. As you've seen, I am a little . . . clumsy with it."

"Clumsy. I guess you could put it that way. I would say you are downright rude," Summer offered.

"Yes, I guess I was. I'm sorry. I brought you this. As an apology. It's good wine," he said, holding up a bottle of Pinot Noir. "Local."

Summer smiled. He'd brought the same brand that she had opened earlier.

"It is very good wine," she said, lifting the empty bottle from her table to show him.

They both chuckled.

"You're wearing a sweatshirt. What happened to your suitcoat?" Summer asked.

Ted looked down at his new apparel and said, "I thought I'd try something new."

"I like it," Summer said. "Would you like to come in for a glass of wine?"

"Ah, no, thank you. I haven't eaten yet. But thank you." He handed her the bottle of wine. "I hope you enjoy your evening."

Summer took the bottle and said, "Thank you."

Ted leisurely walked back to his camper feeling light and unburdened and suddenly very hungry.

He devoured half the lasagna, both rolls, and a cannoli.

How she created such wonderful meals in the small camper perplexed Ted. And to feed so many. He certainly had to respect her abilities. He wrapped the remaining lasagna in the aluminum foil and placed it in his refrigerator.

No longer feeling light, Ted reasoned it not in his best interest to just sit by a campfire and relax. He decided to return Summer's plate to her and then take a walk. Dan insisted he walk daily, and, except for earlier that day, he had been lax in that regard. Dan also cautioned him about eating fatty foods, but that would take more willpower than Ted had yet cultivated.

Ted retrieved a flashlight from the motorhome's glove compartment, one of many habits his father had instilled in him.

"Always keep a light in the box, Teddy," he recalled his father saying. "You never know when you're going to need it."

"Teddy," he said under his breath. Then shook his head. It wasn't the name he hated as much as the way it made him feel. His father expressed it with scorn and distaste for Ted's imperfections.

He stepped down from his camper and peered across the lane to Summer's site. She stood at the back of her van tinkering with something Ted could not see. She had wrapped herself in a multicolored crocheted blanket.

Not wishing to startle her, Ted cleared his throat as he approached her vehicle.

Summer peeked around the corner and smiled.

"You're back," she said.

"Yes. I wanted to return your plate," Ted said.

"You didn't eat it all in one sitting, did you?"

"No, but I wanted to," Ted laughed as he handed her the dish. "It was the best lasagna I ever had. And that cannoli was better than anything you can get in Boston's North End."

"Well, that's high praise. Thank you," Summer said.

"I did eat too much, though. So, I'm going to take a walk and let it settle in," Ted said as he turned to go.

Summer shut the back doors to her van and said, "I'll join you." She took a step forward, then stopped and shook her head. "There I go again. Inviting myself into your life. I'm sorry. I'll let you be."

Ted found her statement encouraging. He hadn't gone about it the right way, but he may have made his point about boundaries.

"No. I'd be happy to have the company," he said before he gave it much thought.

"Okay, then."

Ted's stride far outpaced Summer's gait, but he slowed himself to match hers. That caused him to smile as he remembered having to do the same when he and his wife walked anywhere.

"Are you a professional chef?" Ted asked, breaking the silence.

"I used to be. I went to culinary school about four hours east of here, in Hyde Park," Summer stated, "but that was a lifetime ago."

"What made you stop?"

"When my husband passed away, I needed to attend to his business, and I couldn't do both, so I hung up my pots and pans."

"Do you miss it?"

"Well, I cook for strangers in a campground. What do you think?" Summer snickered.

"Obviously," Ted chuckled. "Did you ever think of opening your own restaurant?"

"Yes. Arnold and I talked about it. But we had other plans that took precedence. What about you? What is it that you do, Teddy?"

"Business law. I have a firm in Massachusetts."

"Uh huh, that makes sense," Summer said.

"What do you mean?"

"Oh, you know, the suits and fancy camper," Summer replied, not wishing to insult him by mentioning his uptight manner. "Do you like what you do?"

"It suits me. Pardon the pun."

"Lawyer humor—I like it. So, you're on vacation then?"

"No. Well, yes."

Summer stopped walking and sent him a quizzical look.

When Ted realized she had stopped, he did also. "What's the matter?"

"'No. Well, yes?' You don't know whether you are on vacation or not?"

Ted looked her in the eyes and replied, "No. I have no idea what I'm doing here."

Summer again began to walk. Ted adopted her pace.

"So, do you have amnesia? Or is there a story here?"

"My daughter threatened to move in with me—her and her family."

"So, you bolted?"

Ted chuckled. "Sort of."

"Look, Teddy. If you don't want to talk about this, just say so. But I'm not well-versed in cryptic conversations. I tend to just open the floodgates and spurt things out."

"Yes, I've noticed."

"So?"

"I had a heart attack, my second one. Marci, my daughter, gave me an ultimatum. Either I give up work and go somewhere to relax, or she and her family would move in with me so she can take care of me." Ted stopped walking and faced Summer. "Can you imagine anything worse than your daughter moving in with you to take care of you, to dictate what you eat, when you sleep, and feed you pills?"

Summer flinched.

Ted continued. "Never mind. I don't want to talk about it. I'm still not sure how I feel about the whole thing. Let's change the subject," Ted said as they walked on. "Are you still running your husband's business?"

"No, I'm finished with that."

"So, what have you been doing since then? Just traveling?"

"No." Summer paused, then blurted, "I had to move in with my parents five years ago to take care of them. Until just recently, it was my full-time job."

Ted halted. "You're making a bad joke, right?"

Summer shook her head.

Ted began to stammer. "I'm sorry, I . . . I'm sure . . . I didn't . . . son of a button."

Summer burst into laughter.

"So, you were joking," Ted said.

"No, I wasn't. I just never heard that saying before. Son of a button? What does that even mean?"

"I don't like to curse. Sometimes I have to catch myself, and things just come out."

"Oh, Teddy. You sure have some strange ideas."

"Me? I have strange ideas? I'm about as strait-laced as they come."

"I know. That's what I mean, poor Teddy," Summer sighed. "Have you ever been comfortable taking help from anyone? Or is this an age thing?"

"What do you mean?"

"You won't let your daughter help you, and any time I try to do something nice, it's agonizing for you. Have you always been this way or just now that you're getting old?"

"I'm not that old."

"You've had two heart attacks. How much older do you think you're going to get?"

"That's a heck of a thing to say to someone."

"You don't like to face reality, do you, Teddy."

Ted stiffened like a starched collar. "Stop calling me Teddy. My name is Ted. And I think I've had enough walking for tonight." He turned and headed back to his campsite.

Exasperation led to anxiety and anxiety led to restlessness. He paced in his motorhome.

The nerve of that woman! Damn it! Why would she say that?

A tiny voice in his head answered his question. *'Because it's true.'*

"Damn it!" he barked.

He brooded for hours before going to bed.

In the morning, Ted finished his routine of showering, shaving, and dressing. He made himself a cup of instant coffee and sat wincing at the bitterness of the murky liquid.

"What am I doing here?" he asked himself.

He looked around the motorhome. It provided a nice living space, comfortable and roomy. He had been sleeping well except for the previous night, which wasn't the fault of the bed. The kitchen had more appliances than he would ever use, and he could take the whole shebang anywhere he wanted. *So why*, he thought, *am I so miserable?*

He considered the previous day. It had been a roller coaster of emotions, none of which he was comfortable with. He missed going to work, dealing with facts and laws and precedence—all tangible things he could make sense of.

Ted suddenly felt a heaviness in his chest. Not like the pressure of a heart attack, but the ache of the emptiness he felt when he thought of Carol, which was often. He missed her dearly. She could always help him make sense of his emotions. She understood him better than anyone in the world, including his parents.

Carol knew the pressure Ted's dad had saddled him with and the self-imposed demand for perfection in his personal and professional life, a nice thought but impossible to live up to. Carol was the only person he ever told about his father showing up one day at his high school gym class. It had been rope-climbing day, and Ted had made the mistake of telling his father the previous week he had been unable to reach the top of the rope. With his father watching from the wooden bleachers in the auditorium, it was Ted's turn to attempt to ring the bell at the top of the rope. Ted had become so nervous he could barely get six feet off the ground. The glare his father directed toward him that day reappeared in Ted's head on many occasions. But with Carol's love and understanding, he could put his relationship with his father in perspective.

He believed Carol was perfect. And she made him a better person.

Ted was the only one who understood why he worked long hours after Carol died. He felt in control in his office, in his conference room, and in his expensive suits. When he wasn't working and without Carol by his side, he felt unprotected and vulnerable.

Summer had been right, Ted thought. He didn't want to face reality. And he found it difficult to accept help from anyone other than his wife.

"So, what now?" Ted whispered.

First things first, he thought. He decided he owed Summer another apology. He had acted like a child, running away like that. Ted admonished himself for being so infantile. How could he fault someone for speaking the unadulterated truth? Didn't he always speak the truth? Wasn't that one of his father's most important rules?

Ted took his coffee and stepped out of the motorhome, but when he looked over at Summer's campsite, her van was gone.

Having no other plan, Ted began to build an early morning fire in the firepit. He used brown paper grocery bags and twigs he picked up from the surrounding area to get the fire started before adding split wood that had been delivered to his lot.

Once the fire roared, he made himself another cup of bad coffee and retrieved the motorhome manual for light reading. He stacked wood in front of his chair to use as a footrest and leaned back.

SUMMER

Just once, Summer, would you think before you speak? she thought to herself after Ted walked away.

She spent the remainder of the evening trying to soothe her angst through meditation, but as hard as she tried, shame kept creeping into her thoughts.

Her body jumped from the bed as she woke the next morning from a dream. Anxiety seeped through her like spilled oil in a pristine ocean. Summer tried to recall the dream that caused her uneasiness but could not.

She sat on the side of her bed, stunned. She couldn't remember the last time she woke feeling anything but excited for the day ahead. Even while caring for her parents, she woke with enthusiasm and eagerness. That day, however, she felt dread, and it unnerved her.

Before doing anything, Summer reached for her Nordic rune stones for clarity. She used the set as a tool for divination. The modern set of stones featured the second century Germanic alphabet, Futhark, and came with a guidebook for interpreting their meanings.

The idea was to ask a question, cast the stones, and interpret them as they lay. The guidebook described multiple layouts and formats. She could cast one stone or many.

Summer wanted only one. She put flame to her sage smudge stick and placed it in a conch shell. She breathed deeply, then asked, "Where is this uneasiness coming from, and what do I need to know about it?"

Reaching into the black velvet bag, Summer randomly picked a stone and placed it on a white embroidered handkerchief. The cloth had belonged to her mother.

She had pulled Nauthiz, the ancient symbol for constraint. She knew the stone well. She had received it many times before. It represented her stunted growth which sometimes resulted in her weaknesses being thrust upon others. According to the *Book of Runes*, Nauthiz calls for restraint and a clear notion that work needs to be done on the self. It also suggests using adversity with good humor and perseverance to grow.

Summer suddenly remembered the dream she had awakened from. She sat on the edge of a swamp. The sun shone on a cloudless day, and insects circled her but left her untouched. She felt invincible until she noticed an alligator in the water. Its eyes concentrated on her as it inched closer and closer until it was at the water's edge. She tried to get up and run, but she couldn't move. The gator waded through the tall grass and lay at her feet, mouth open, still staring into her eyes. Then it moved suddenly. That's when she woke.

She retrieved her book about the spiritual meanings of animals. When she found the page referring to alligators, she read:

In Native American lore, the alligator symbolizes, among other things, the need to reserve judgment of others. Especially if the others in question are serious and rigid.

"Well, Summer, you shouldn't have needed the universe to help you with this one. When are you going to learn?" She chuckled. "My higher self is a trickster."

And then the notion hit her. *Maybe I'm not here to help Teddy? Maybe he is here to help me be my best self?*

While sipping her herbal tea, Summer worked on apology scenarios. Always her first instinct, she thought about making him a lavish dessert. But Ted had already had two heart attacks, and she certainly didn't wish to contribute to his third.

Wine was out of the question, too, although Summer considered wine a natural remedy for anxiety. Antioxidants were, after all, good for the heart. Of course, she based her belief on studies she only partially read. But wine would seem too much like re-gifting.

She assumed Ted would not be receptive to flowers.

Then she thought, *I don't need to get him anything. I'll just knock on his door and be direct. I'll apologize for suggesting he was old and might not live much longer. Damn it, why can't I just keep my mouth shut?*

"No, that won't do it either," she sighed. "But I think I know what will."

Summer finished her tea, took a shower, and got dressed. Her uneasiness had vanished, and she was eager to begin her day. She noticed a light on in Ted's trailer when she drove away.

An hour and a half later, Summer backed her van into her campsite. Across the way, Ted sat next to the firepit, his feet propped up on a pile of wood. His chin rested on his chest, and he held a book against his body. He was sound asleep. The fire had burned down, producing little flame.

She smiled at the sight.

Quietly, Summer unpacked her van of several grocery bags, a large box, and a white plastic bag with the words Thank you! inked on it.

Once she put the groceries away, she picked up the large box and the white bag and headed to see Ted. She decided that if he were still sleeping, she would just leave the items for him to see when he woke.

She walked on the crushed stone driveway as quietly as she could. When Ted didn't budge, she placed the packages next to the motorhome stairs and was about to turn around and go back to her camper when she decided to place another log or two on the fire to keep Ted warm while he slept.

As she laid the second log in the pit, she heard, "It works better if you place the logs like a teepee. I learned that in the Boy Scouts."

Summer turned to see Ted weary eyed but smiling.

"True, but if you lay them flat, you get fewer flying embers," she replied.

Ted took his feet off the wood stack, lay the motorhome manual on the ground, and sat up straight in his chair.

"Is that true?" he asked.

"I have no idea," Summer replied. "Someone once told me that."

The uncertainty resulted in laughter from them both.

"Did you need something?" Ted asked.

"Uh, yes. I did," Summer said. "I need to apologize to you."

"No," Ted said. "I need to apologize to you again."

"No, you don't," said Summer. "I had no right to say those things last night. Your life is none of my business, and I shouldn't presume to know anything about you. I have a bad habit of projecting my baggage onto others. It's something I am trying to work on—unsuccessfully, as you can see."

"I acted like a child," Ted said. "Me, a sixty-seven-year-old child."

"You are not sixty-seven." Summer seemed surprised.

Ted unconsciously revealed the sweet smile that his wife could not resist and one he hadn't brandished since her death.

"Yes, I am," Ted said, "but it's very nice of you to feign surprise."

"Teddy, I don't feign. I just don't think it's fair that men age so much more gently than us women."

Ted grinned again. He noticed the items sitting by his camper and asked, "What are those?"

"One is a peace offering. The other? Well, you'll see," Summer grinned.

Ted got up and walked over to the packages. The large box displayed a picture of a coffee maker with the words *Mr. Coffee*.

"Is it really a coffee maker?" Ted asked excitedly.

"It is. And before you say that you can't accept it, I—"

"I'll accept it," Ted quickly interrupted. "I can't take another day of this instant sludge."

"Open the bag," Summer urged.

Ted reached into the bag and retrieved a pound of coffee.

"I guessed that you didn't have any of that either," Summer smirked.

"No, I did bring coffee," he answered, "just nothing to brew it in." He laughed. "Thank you very much. But you didn't have to."

"I know I didn't. But I wanted to. There's one more thing in the bag," Summer motioned for him to look.

Ted's eyes scrunched, and then he reached back into the bag. He pulled out a white t-shirt.

"I know how much you like them," Summer giggled.

Ted held the t-shirt up and released a belly laugh. Pink and purple frolicking unicorns decorated the front of the shirt.

"It's stylish. It will go perfectly with my Brooks Brothers suit." Ted meticulously folded the t-shirt as if to put it on display, then said, "How about I make us some coffee and we sit by the fire for a bit?"

"I'd like that," Summer replied. "I'll go get my coffee cup and a chair while you make the coffee."

Not only did Summer get her cup and chair, but she also quickly threw together a platter of grapes, strawberries, bananas, and melon, all of which she had just bought. By the time she returned to the campfire, the coffee was ready.

She placed the fruit platter and napkins on the table between Ted's chair and hers.

"Do you use cream or sugar?" Ted asked hesitantly.

"No, just black," she replied.

"That's good, because I don't have any."

"Mmmm, this is good coffee. I'll be honest. I was going to be polite, but I didn't expect to like it."

"My one and only job in the house was to make the morning coffee. My wife did everything else."

"Tell me about her, your wife."

Ted's eyes softened. "Her name was Carol. She was the most beautiful woman I've ever known, inside and out. She was smart, funny, and, boy, could she carry a tune."

He spoke as if from another dimension, one where Carol still stood next to him, holding his hand. Nothing could sway his blissful smile, not that Summer wanted to. "She was a music teacher. A complete opposite personality to me. That's what drew me to her."

"How did you meet?" Summer asked.

"We met at a Bruce Springsteen concert just before Christmas in 1980. I went with a friend who was meeting his girlfriend there," Ted chuckled.

"Oh, don't tell me you stole his girlfriend," Summer snickered.

"No, I stole his girlfriend's girlfriend. My friend Jay was dating a girl named Allison. Carol had gone to the concert with Allison, and I had gone with Jay. So, naturally, we hung out together. That night changed my life. Jay and Allison broke up two weeks later. Carol and I were married two years later."

"How timely for you," Summer said.

"I don't know. I've always had the feeling that if we hadn't met at that concert, we would have met somewhere else. Like we were meant to be." Ted mused as he popped a strawberry into his mouth.

Summer perked up. "Do you mean like divine intervention?"

"I don't know what that means." Ted shook his head.

"Do you believe that all things happen for a reason?" Summer asked.

"No," Ted said abruptly. "What reason could there be for Carol to die from breast cancer? No. Sometimes things just happen." Ted grew somber.

"How long has she been gone?"

"Almost five years."

"I'm sorry. She sounds like she was a wonderful person. And your daughter? Is she more like your wife or you?"

"Unfortunately, Marci tapped into the wrong bloodline. She is very much like me, although she has her mother's eyes and heart."

Summer sensed that Ted had finished talking. She reached for a piece of melon and slid it into her mouth.

After a brief silence, Summer said, "My husband made candles. My father couldn't stand Arnold. He always said he couldn't understand how anyone could put so much energy into making a product that didn't do anything but *stink up a room*. Arnold was sweet and had a beautiful heart until it gave out on him fifteen years ago."

"Your husband had a heart attack?" Ted asked.

"Yes. Three heart attacks, actually. The third one killed him."

"That's why you said that last night? About already having two heart attacks?" Ted asked.

"Yes, I guess so. I'm sorry. Sometimes I speak before I think. Just because it happened to him doesn't mean it will happen to you," Summer said.

"Right," Ted murmured and grew quiet.

They sat in silence, both staring into the fire.

Then Summer asked, "Do you think you'll go back to work, Teddy?"

"I don't know. My daughter was pretty clear about it. So was Dan, my doctor. They don't think I should. But what would I do? It's all I know."

"Well, we all have to change. Life is nothing but change. I, for one, have decided I would like to go to the Rock & Roll Hall of Fame. That's where I was headed before I changed my mind and came directly here."

Ted laughed. "Ohio. You were headed to Ohio?"

"Yes. What's so funny about Ohio?"

"I was headed to the Pro Football Hall of Fame, which is in . . . "

"Ohio," Summer finished with a cackle.

"What made you stop here in New York?" Ted asked.

"The wine. And you?"

"That monstrosity of a motorhome. But I'm getting better at maneuvering it," Ted chuckled.

"Why did you buy something so big?" Summer asked.

"I don't know. I like my comforts, I suppose."

"I like simplicity," Summer offered.

"But you do have quite a kitchen setup in that van. That took some doing." Ted inquisitively tilted his head.

"Yes, I suppose that's where *my* comforts lie."

"Is that how you make a living? Cooking for people in the campgrounds you stay at?"

Summer nearly doubled up with laughter. "You think . . . "—her laugh more of a hoot—"you think I . . . cook . . . for money?" She couldn't stop herself. She continued to chortle.

Ted looked confused and a bit skittish. "Why is that so funny?"

Summer quieted her laugh and sat shaking her head. "Oh, Teddy. That was funny. No, I don't cook for these people to make money. I don't even charge them. I cook because I love to cook. And they eat because they like my food."

"But what about the coffee can?" Ted asked.

"Look. Some people, like you, for instance, don't feel right accepting something for nothing. So, I leave the can out, and they feel better about eating my food."

"But what about the cost?"

"Teddy, I have more money than I would need in my next five lifetimes. I've got to spend it on something. So, I spend it on doing what I love to do, which is to cook for people."

Ted raised an eyebrow when Summer mentioned having more money than she could ever spend. He glanced over to her tiny trailer and then back to her.

"I bought her when I sold my husband's business six months ago." Summer said, looking at her Shasta camper. "She's vintage. She cost me a bundle, but I love her. Then I found the van and had both customized to my specifications."

"What was your husband's business?" Ted asked.

"I told you. He made candles," Summer said, waiting for Ted to put the facts together. She figured, him a business lawyer from Massachusetts, he would have heard about the sale.

She watched as Ted processed the information. Then he raised his eyebrows. "Your husband, Arnold? Arnold Case? Of Case Candles? The largest candle and gift business in the country? That's the guy you married who made candles?"

Summer nodded her head the entire time Ted ranted. "Well, he wasn't so big when we got married. He had a small shop in Vermont. But it grew."

"I'll say it grew. I've used his business model when advising clients. Every business lawyer does. Well, I'll be a son of a duck."

Summer burst into laughter again. "I just love your idioms."

Ted suddenly looked away and went quiet.

"Teddy? Are you all right?" Summer asked.

"Ah, yes. I'm just shocked. And I feel a bit foolish."

"Why are you shocked? You're in business law. You must deal with this kind of thing all the time," Summer said.

"I've been reading about you in business magazines. How you took over after your husband passed away. How, last year, you sold Case Candles for a whopping 1.75 billion dollars!" Then Ted cocked his head and said, "I thought you said you've been taking care of your parents for the last five years."

"I was."

"Well, how were you able to do both? Take care of your parents and run the company?"

"Oh, after the first few years, I didn't really need to run the company. Arnold had put together a very competent organization—a group of lovely, smart, and now very well-off individuals who loved him very much. They helped me fill Arnold's shoes as the company's figurehead at first, but they didn't need me for long. I mostly represented stability for the shareholders. The employees did all the heavy lifting."

"Why is it I don't recognize you? I've seen many newspaper and magazine articles about your company and read every one of them. But I've never seen a picture of you, with or without your husband."

"Oh, God, no. I wouldn't allow it. Arnold didn't understand my position, either. He insisted it would be good for business to parade us in the media as a couple. But I don't trust the media, so I didn't want any part of that."

"What about children? Do you have any?"

"No. We exhausted all our options, but it never worked out for us. By the time we admitted to ourselves we could never have children of our own, the system thought us too old to adopt," Summer said.

"I'm sorry, I didn't mean to pry."

"Not at all. It's a perfectly normal question, one that I have made my peace with."

Silence seemed called for, so they sat listening to the crackle of the fire and the birds chirping.

"Well," said Summer, the first to break the stillness, "I have some chicken to marinate." She stood and placed her empty coffee cup on the table beside the fruit platter. "Thank you for the coffee. And the conversation. You're getting much better at this socializing thing," Summer said as she folded her chair, picked up her cup, and began to leave.

"What about the fruit?" Ted asked.

"Keep it. It's good for you. Maybe you should take a picture of it and send it to your daughter so she won't worry so much about you," Summer said as she walked back to her trailer.

TED

Twenty minutes after Summer left, Ted's telephone rang.

"Good morning, Marci," Ted answered the call.

"Good morning, Dad. What's up with the picture of fruit?"

Ted chuckled. "I just wanted you to see that I am eating healthy and you don't have to worry about me."

"Boy, you really don't want us moving in with you, do you?" Marci sniggered.

"I've come to realize that wouldn't be the worst thing in the world, and maybe someday, when I'm ninety, you might have to do that," Ted said.

"What's gotten into you, Dad? You're being awfully agreeable. Is that fresh air making you light-headed?"

"Oh, Marci. It's a pity you are so much like me. I'm sorry, pumpkin. You are doomed."

Marci released the sweet girlish laugh Ted remembered so fondly from her childhood.

"I love you, Dad."

"I love you, too, pumpkin. We'll talk again soon."

A SPLASH OF CONTENTMENT

SUMMER

Her hands busy mixing oatmeal raisin cookie dough, Summer reflected on her morning. She had awakened with a feeling of restlessness and a heavy heart, but as the sun rose, so had her spirits—largely due to her conversation with Ted.

She had come to think of herself as a somewhat enlightened person, one who understood the scope of the universe and her place in it. She endeavored to live her best life, one of giving, caring, and loving.

She chuckled to herself, *I guess I'm not as enlightened as I thought I was. I've still got a long way to go. Who would've thought it would take a business lawyer to hit me over the head?*

As she dropped spoonsful of cookie dough onto a sheet pan, Summer recalled the look on Ted's face as he spoke about his wife. The image made her smile.

She had grossly underestimated him, she thought. And she was frustrated with herself because, much like her father had always done, she judged Ted before she even knew him. He was not the uptight, unyielding man he seemed at first impression. *I think it's a shield, not arrogance. And he's not as confident as he first comes off. Who am I to judge?* she thought. *I know a little bit about hiding my own emotions.*

With the first pan of cookies baking, Summer began to prepare mashed cauliflower. Fifteen years before, she never would have thought about substituting cauliflower for mashed potatoes but found it a very satisfying side dish. She wondered if Arnold would have thought the same.

A tinge of groundless guilt invaded her thoughts. Because of the rich foods she used to make, Summer had felt culpable for Arnold's heart attack even though the doctor said his death was partially due to a hereditary heart defect. Arnold loved her cooking, and she loved cooking for him. It was one of her life's greatest joys to watch him take pleasure in her pork chops or revel in her risotto.

A decent cook himself, he surprised her now and then with dinner. She found herself missing his New England boiled dinner and the baked beans made using his mother's recipe. *He was so proud of them*, Summer recalled.

Arnold was everything Summer's father was not: sensitive, funny, sociable, and caring. And most of the time, Arnold didn't have a problem talking about his feelings. She could count on one hand the number of major disagreements they had during their thirty-two years together.

Although Summer's mother made the most of her own marriage, Summer knew she harbored sadness beneath her surface. But her mother never allowed Summer a peek into her innermost thoughts. Instead, she shared platitudes or what Summer perceived as platitudes—"I packed my own bag." "A choice made is a choice lived." "Not all love can be seen."

Could I have been wrong? Was my mother happy with her life? How can I know? We never talked about happiness. Summer pondered.

The things I think I know are not necessarily things that are. Why is that so hard for me to grasp?

As Summer's thoughts preoccupied her mind, her hands kept busy. Before she knew it, she had prepared the entire night's meal and cleaned her kitchen, and the clock hadn't yet struck noon.

Sitting down with a cup of tea, Summer retrieved her list of things to do. She'd created the list four days before when she decided to extend her stay in the campground. It included exploring parks with gorges, waterfalls, and rivers; visiting the farmers market, animal preserve, Museum of Imagination, and multiple wineries and cider houses in the area. She had chosen to leave breweries off her list since she wasn't much of a beer drinker and didn't include any restaurants to avoid restricting her choices when the time came to treat herself.

As she read through her list, she had a notion to ask if Ted would like to join her for a day of exploring. Then she dismissed the thought. Then she rethought her dismissal of the thought.

When did you get so indecisive, Summer? she asked herself.

She finished her tea and strolled over to Ted's trailer. He answered after several knocks.

Summer saw that Ted's hair was uncharacteristically disheveled. "I didn't wake you again, did I, Teddy?"

"No. Come in. I was trying to hook up the campground's cable to my television. I've never been good with electronics." Ted brushed his fingers through his hair.

"I can't help you there. I don't own a television," Summer said as she climbed the stairs into the motorhome. Pulled away from the wall, the living room television mounted to a swing arm. It stuck out at an angle large enough to cut the room almost in half. Summer saw electrical and cable cords dangling from behind and several manuals lying open on the living room couch.

Ted cast her an inquisitive look. "Really? No television at all?" he questioned.

"Really. The things that roll around in my head are usually much more entertaining than anything I could watch on TV." She paused. "Other than setting up that boob tube, what are your plans for the day?"

"Ah, watching it, I guess," Ted replied.

"What would your friend, the doctor, think about that?" Summer raised her brows. "I propose you come with me to one of the many state parks in the area. We could go for a walk, separately if you prefer, and then reward ourselves with a glass of wine at a local winery. What do you say?"

"Ah, well, I don't know."

"Come on, Teddy. What are your alternatives? To wade through a bunch of daytime TV programs?"

Summer watched as Ted processed his choices.

"Are you a good driver?" Ted asked.

"My father taught me to drive when I was twelve years old. I've never gotten a ticket, and the only accident I ever had was someone smashing their door into mine in the grocery store parking lot. Would you like my full resume?"

Ted rolled his eyes. "All right, all right. It was just a question. When would you want to leave?"

"In about twenty minutes?"

"Okay. I'll go."

"Good. Do you have any good walking shoes?" Summer asked.

Ted looked at his feet. He wore his black wing-tip oxfords.

Summer glanced at his feet, frowned, then said, "We'll stop at a shoe store and get you some decent walking sneakers. I'll see you in twenty minutes."

Summer drove them to the same department store Ted had previously gone to. While there, he bought sneakers, jeans, a couple of shirts, and a baseball cap. He arranged with the salesperson to wear the jeans, one of the shirts, and sneakers out of the store.

"You look like a whole different person, Teddy," Summer said as they loaded themselves back into her van.

"It's been a long time since I didn't have to dress for work. I guess if I have to change, my wardrobe will have to change with me."

"That's the spirit. I thought we might head south to Taughannock Falls State Park. I hear the gorge is beautiful."

"You're in the driver's seat. Lead on," Ted said with a wave of his hand.

"You know," Summer said after a few miles, "I've been thinking about something."

"Oh? What's that?"

"You said you met your wife at a Bruce Springsteen concert in 1980?"

"That's right. Just before Christmas."

"Was the concert at Boston Garden?"

"Yes, it was. He put on a heck of a show."

"I know," Summer said, "Arnold and I were there."

Ted turned to Summer. "No. You were there?"

Summer nodded. "In the first set, Bruce wore a blue denim shirt with jeans. He opened with 'Born to Run' and closed the second set with 'Rosalita.'"

"And he played 'Santa Claus is Coming to Town' during his encore," Ted said. "The whole place erupted."

"I still have my t-shirt from that night," Summer laughed.

"That was forty-two years ago," Ted pondered. "What are the odds?"

"Pretty crazy, right?"

"Yes, pretty crazy."

They drove in silence, Summer reflecting on that night when she first became pregnant. The memory sparked both joy, then anguish.

"It's a fleeting thing, isn't it?" Ted quietly said.

"What is?" Summer asked.

"Happiness," he responded soberly.

Summer's instinct was to delve into the world of metaphysics and discuss her opinion that the soul lives on and they will see their loved ones again. She wished to impress upon him that she thinks everything happens for a reason. But she stopped herself. Her beliefs were her beliefs, and she didn't think this was the time to share them.

So, instead, Summer said, "Yes, it is. That's why we need to treat every moment as if it's our last." Taking her right hand off the wheel, Summer spread her fingers and scooped a handful of air, resulting in a closed fist. "We need to latch on to happiness and spread it around every chance we get."

"That's a nice thought," Ted said, "but very difficult to do."

"Nobody said it would be easy. Besides, we only need to try. We're not expected to be perfect," Summer explained.

They completed the drive with small talk, pulling into Taughannock Falls State Park at almost 1:30 pm. Being early spring, visitors numbered far less than would fill the park in the coming months. Still, there were many families with children, dogs, and picnic lunches roaming about.

Summer and Ted chose to walk the Gorge Trail, approximately one mile long and a fairly easy hike. Keeping a comfortable pace, they walked the pathway until they came to the first of two waterfalls. According to Summer's earlier research about the park, the water of Lower Falls flowed over a layer of hard Tully limestone, keeping its stair-step form, before reaching the much softer Moscow formation beneath it, resulting in a more weathered surface. Then the water gathered in a pool before continuing downstream.

The rush of the water soothed Summer's soul.

"It's beautiful, isn't it?" Summer asked.

It's quite calming, the sound of running water, Summer thought.

TED

Children waded in the shallow water while others played fetch with a Golden Retriever nearby. Summer and Ted found an unoccupied bench and lingered to watch and listen.

"Let's go in," Summer jumped from the bench.

"What?"

"Come on, Teddy. Take those bright white sneakers off and get your feet wet."

"No, thank you. I'm perfectly happy sitting here and watching. You go ahead, though," Ted said.

"Don't you ever do anything impulsive? What are you afraid of?"

"I'm not afraid of anything. I just don't want to get wet."

"Why? Give me one good reason why you shouldn't put your feet into that pristine water and enjoy what nature has provided," Summer said as she took off her sandals.

"The flu," Ted responded.

Summer glared at Ted. "You would become a medical marvel. The first person in history to catch the flu by sticking a toe in a pool of fresh running water."

Summer placed her sandals under the bench and eased herself into the water.

Ted watched as a smile filled Summer's face. She held her arms out straight and twirled like a little girl in a ballerina tutu. A child nearby mocked her movement, and before long, several of the children twirled in unison with Summer, all of them laughing.

Ted smiled, then removed his sneakers, folded his socks, and placed them under the bench. He rolled his pant legs evenly up to his knees.

The water felt cold and invigorating. His bare feet found the occasional pebble, but they mostly landed on soft sand. He stood, facing the steps of the hard limestone, wondering how long it took for the water to carve the falls. He contemplated the ever-changing nature of his surroundings. How he couldn't see the transformation with the naked eye but knew it was happening.

He felt a splash of water on the back of his neck and turned. Summer grinned, a mischievous look in her eyes.

Making sure no children would be affected, Ted reached down into the water and reciprocated with a hefty handful of water toward Summer. She tried to shield herself with her hands to no avail.

"Truce," she screamed.

"Truce," he replied.

"What made you change your mind?" Summer asked.

You, Ted almost said. Instead, he shrugged his shoulders and turned his face to the sun. He stood with his eyes closed, basking in the warmth, and listened to the water flow around him. He wasn't sure how much time had passed before he heard Summer ask, "Are you ready to move on?"

Donning their shoes, they walked upstream alongside Taughannock Creek before reaching the highest single-drop waterfall of the Northeast, Taughannock Falls. Dropping 215 feet higher than Niagara Falls, Taughannock Falls had eroded roughly 400 feet of shale to create the gorge over time.

As Ted read the information on the kiosk at the base of the falls, a realization occurred to him. Nothing on this earth escapes change. Of course, intellectually, he already knew that, but he never really accepted it when it came to him personally. For so long, his life had been exactly what he wanted it to be.

"Are you all right, Teddy?" Summer asked.

"Yes, why do you ask?"

"You look worried."

Ted chuckled. "I was just contemplating the meaning of life," he replied.

Summer chuckled. "Well, when you really want to know, just ask me. But we might need a few bottles of wine for that conversation."

"Are you telling me you know the answer to the oldest question of mankind?" Ted laughed.

"Yes, I believe I do. And the answer isn't as complicated as you might think," Summer said, her face as serious as a pin-less grenade.

"Don't tell me. It's world peace," Ted laughed.

"No, that would be the result if we all understood the meaning of life and lived accordingly," Summer said.

"All right, I'll bite," Ted said. "What, in your opinion, is the meaning of life?"

Summer looked Ted in the eyes. "Are you a spiritual man, Teddy?"

Ted ceased smiling. "My parents brought me up as a Catholic, but I wouldn't say I'm religious."

"That's not what I asked you," Summer said. "I asked you if you are a spiritual man."

"I don't understand the question," Ted replied.

"I know." Summer shifted the topic of conversation. "What do you say we head out? If we leave now, we'll still have time to stop at a winery."

"Sure," Ted said, confused by her sudden shift.

They decided to stop at Cayuga Cask and Keg, a combination winery/brewery close to the campground. That way, they wouldn't have far to drive when finished.

Summer chose to sample an aromatic Riesling while Ted switched gears and ordered a draft ale. Rather than stay in the tasting room and learn about the history of the local business, Summer and Ted found an unoccupied picnic table outside, overlooking the lake.

They sat on the same side of the table so each could enjoy the view.

After a few moments, Summer asked, "Teddy, do you think we are destined to become our parents?"

Ted was beginning to understand that, when in Summer's presence, he should expect the unexpected. It wasn't that Ted was incapable of talking about personal issues, but he had never done so with anyone except his wife.

However, this was a question he had recently reflected upon. So, he jumped in.

"I think it would take a very strong personality to escape the possibility," he replied.

Summer sat up straight and eyed Ted. "Wow, that was . . . huh . . . deep. Almost like you rehearsed it."

Ted took a sip of his ale. "It's something I've been thinking a lot about lately. Why do you ask?"

Summer paused before speaking. "My father was an extremely judgmental person."

Ted nodded, as if he understood completely.

Summer continued, "I told you he didn't like my husband. Well, he never gave him a chance. He decided from the moment they met that Arnold was a weak man. Of course, he wasn't, but it didn't matter to my father."

"Even after all of his success?" Ted asked.

"My father attributed it to luck and not hard work. It caused irreparable damage to me and my father's relationship right up to the end. Not that we had the best of relationships before then."

Ted nodded again.

"But the worst of it is, as hard as I try, his judgmental nature still comes through in me. Not as drastically as it did him, but it's still there." Summer sat with her hands wrapped around her wine glass and her head bowed.

Ted reflexively rested his hand on Summer's arm and said, "You are the least judgmental person I have ever met. So what if you make assumptions now and then? Like you told me, we're not expected to be perfect, right?"

When Ted became conscious of his hand on Summer's arm, he quickly removed it.

Summer smiled. "I suppose you're right. If I were perfect, I wouldn't need to be here."

"What do you mean, wouldn't need to be here?"

"Oh, nothing. That's a whole different conversation," Summer said.

Before giving it much thought, Ted said, "My father preached perfection. He was a difficult man. He would have made a great drill sergeant had he gotten the chance, but the army wouldn't accept him."

Ted saw the question on Summer's face and responded.

"He had asthma. He had it all his life. So, because he couldn't live the life he wanted to live, he tried to turn my brother and me into his own perfect little army. No slouching, no swearing, no laughing, no playing. If it weren't for my mother, well, I don't know what we would have done. She was a saint."

"Most men's mothers are," Summer mused. "So, you have a brother?"

"I do. Harold. He's three years older than me."

"Where does he live? Do you get to see him?" Summer seemed pleased.

"He's in Germany." Ted paused. "He's a retired colonel of the US Army."

Summer didn't say a word. She only watched Ted's expression turn to pride.

"He was always the stronger brother," Ted said with a smile.

"Oh, I don't know about that," Summer said. "A very wise man once told me that it would take a strong personality to avoid becoming our parents."

Ted straightened his back, lifted his head, and turned to Summer. She lifted her glass of wine and smirked. Ted picked up his beer mug and tapped her glass before taking a sip.

As she set her wine glass on the table, Summer said, "Did you know that grapevines possess both male and female reproductive characteristics? They self-pollinate. Isn't that fascinating?"

Ted chuckled. "Someone could get whiplash when having a conversation with you, Summer."

꙳ ꙳

As he stood with his plate in hand, Ted thought the dinner line seemed short that night. It usually stretched out of Summer's campsite and continued into the lane that separated Ted and Summer's lots. That night it barely reached the edge of the site. Not knowing what meal Summer had prepared, he tried to discern the contents by the odors wafting around him.

He picked up the scent of garlic, as he did most nights, and something herbal. But he could not separate the individual seasonings.

When Summer saw him waiting, she smiled.

He made small talk with the others in line, the subject heavily leaning toward Summer's cooking abilities. When he reached the front of the queue, he tossed a ten-dollar bill into the coffee can and smiled.

Summer shook her head and chuckled. "Herb-grilled chicken, mashed cauliflower, and balsamic-glazed asparagus. Finished with an oatmeal-raisin cookie."

"It looks delicious. Thank you," Ted said.

"I'm happy you finally made it to dinner," Summer said.

The following night Summer served poached salmon with shallot and low-salt soy sauce on a bed of steamed spinach and kale. A cottage cheese fruit tarte completed the meal.

The next night she filled the plates with grilled Caesar salad, Cajun spiced shrimp, and roasted mixed vegetables. Egg custard rounded out the menu.

Each night Ted watched the dinner line get shorter and shorter.

When he woke the next morning, Ted knew he had to say something. But he didn't wish to sound ungrateful. With a cup of coffee in hand, Ted walked across the lane and knocked on Summer's door.

"Good morning, Teddy." Summer smiled.

"Good morning, Summer. Have you got a minute?" Ted asked.

"I've got nothing but minutes," she replied. "Do you want to come in or sit outside?"

"Let's sit outside. Your camper makes me feel like a giant," Ted said.

Summer brought her coffee, and the two sat at her table.

"I have to ask you something," Ted said, "and I don't mean to sound self-centered or ungrateful."

Summer grew serious. "Oh. Okay. What is it?"

Ted took a deep breath, then said, "Have you altered your dinner menu because of me?"

Summer burst into laughter. "Jesus, Teddy, that's what you wanted to ask me? I thought something was wrong."

"Well, there is if you've changed the way you cook because of me," Ted said.

Summer shook her head and sighed.

"Let me tell you a story. When I was a young girl, I watched a television show called *The Galloping Gourmet*. The star of the cooking show was a man named Graham Kerr. I just loved him. He was funny, entertaining, and he made me fall in love with cooking. Of course, I grew up watching Julia Child too, but it was Graham Kerr that I really enjoyed. He loved butter, wine, and cream. His show didn't last long, and he had many critics, but I didn't care.

"Later in Graham's life, mostly because of his wife's medical condition, he turned to healthy cooking. I tried to get excited about it, but I couldn't. There have been many times since Arnold passed away that I wished I could have embraced the healthy Graham Kerr. So, to answer your question, yes and no. You did remind me that, when it comes to food, too much of a good thing is too much. And, yes, maybe your heart attacks played a role in my grocery shopping, but it wasn't only you. I don't want to contribute to anyone else having a heart attack either."

"Well, you're losing your audience," Ted said.

"Excuse me?"

"I'm sure you've noticed that the dinner line has shortened considerably since grilled chicken night."

Summer pursed her lips and scowled. "I've noticed."

"What are you going to do about it?"

"It depends."

"On what?"

"Do you promise to eat responsibly?" Summer asked.

Ted put his hand on his chest and said, "I promise. Now, what's for dinner?" He laughed.

"How do you feel about smoked spareribs?"

"I could eat a dozen," Ted professed.

Summer wagged her finger at Ted and shook her head.

SHOWERED WITH MEMORIES

TED

"Marci's coming to visit," Ted blurted.

"How nice for you. When?" Summer asked.

"Tomorrow. Her, Frank, and the boys. What am I going to do?"

"What do you mean, what are you going to do?"

Ted threw another log on the fire.

"I don't entertain people," he said, shifting in his chair, his nerves clearly getting the best of him.

"You're entertaining me right now—in more ways than one," Summer laughed. "You are literally squirming in your chair. Relax. Why are you so nervous? You invited them, didn't you?"

"Yes, I did," he replied, his tone full of dread.

"I thought you had a good relationship with your daughter."

"I do!" Ted shifted in his chair again. "But what do I do with the boys? For a whole weekend?"

"How old are they?"

Ted paused, then said, "Frankie Jr. is thirteen. Casey is five years younger, eight."

"Take them to Taughannock Falls or one of the other parks around here for a hike. Maybe the zoo? Or a museum? There's a lot to do around here."

Ted stood and paced. "Yes, the park. That's perfect. It will eat up half the day."

Her eyes pinched, she tracked Ted's movement. "Eat up? Teddy, what's the matter with you? You're acting like you never hung out with your grandkids before."

Ted stopped pacing and faced Summer. Sounding embarrassed, he said, "That's because I haven't."

"What? How can that be?"

"I mean, I have, but Carol was always there to steer the conversation and entertain them. Since she's been gone, I've only seen them on holidays when there's lots of people around. So, no, I haven't spent much one-on-one time with them in five years."

"Then this will give you a great opportunity to get to know them. They're just kids, Teddy, not a judge and jury. Besides, your daughter and son-in-law are going to be here, too, right?"

"Yes."

"Then relax. Kids are just small people, Teddy. They're just trying to find their way like the rest of us."

"I'm just not qualified to help them," Ted whispered under his breath, not intending Summer to hear.

"Of course you are! My goodness, Teddy, you are a terrific person. An excellent role model. Those kids are lucky to have you."

Embarrassed by being overheard, Ted glanced away.

Summer continued. "Listen, if you need anything, I am a traveling entertainment center."

Ted turned and met her gaze with a raised eyebrow.

"Oh, no. That didn't come out right. I meant I have the equipment to entertain . . .."

Ted began to chuckle.

"That didn't sound appropriate either, did it?"

Ted's chuckle triggered Summer. While laughing, she said, "I just meant, I know how to have fun and I . . ."

Ted began to laugh as he hadn't in years. The sound carried down the lane and took most of his anxiety with it.

Summer shook her head and, giving up altogether, threw her hands in the air.

At nearly nine Friday night, Summer and Ted sat sipping wine around the campfire when Marci's red Grand Caravan pulled into Ted's campsite.

Ted stood and waved as Frank shut the lights off and the family stepped out of the van. Ted greeted Frank at the car and shook his hand. "You made good time."

"That's because he wouldn't let us stop for anything," Frankie Jr. belted. "I gotta go to the bathroom."

"Hey there, Frankie. Casey. Up the stairs and to the right," Ted pointed.

Frankie Jr. hurried inside, and Casey followed.

It had been a couple months since Ted had seen the kids and then only quickly when Marci had made some excuse to stop by his house and inspect the contents of his refrigerator. Ted was reminded how quickly children's appearances can change. Frankie Jr., contrary to his namesake, shared his mother's soft, symmetrical appearance. In turn, Casey bore his father's chiseled facial features.

Marci came around the side of the van carrying a pillow and blanket.

"Hi, sweetheart. Let me take those." Ted took the items and kissed her on the cheek. "Oh, Marci, Frank, this is Summer," he said as he turned to go inside. "Summer, this is my daughter and her husband."

"It's so nice to meet you. Your father talks about you and the boys all the time," Summer said.

"It's very nice to meet you, Summer," Marci replied.

Ted brought the blanket and pillow inside and while there showed the boys how to use the motorhome toilet. "When you want to flush, just step on that pedal down there. And be careful not to use too much toilet paper, okay? We don't want to be clogging up the system here," Ted smiled.

Frankie Jr. pressed the toilet pedal and watched as a flap on the bottom of the tank opened while water rinsed the inside, then swirled down through the open hole. He let up on the pedal and smiled as the flap closed.

"Can I try now?" Casey asked.

"Sure thing, Casey. But remember, we don't want to waste water either. Go ahead. Give it a try," Ted said.

Casey grinned as the bottom valve opened and the water circled down the drain.

"That's pretty cool. What else do you have in here?" Frankie Jr. asked.

"Well, I've got this television over here in the living room."

The boys each plopped into a recliner as Ted showed them how to work the remote control. By the time Ted got back to the door, Summer and Marci were sipping wine together by the fire and Frank had unpacked the van into a pile on the ground next to the door.

Still standing at the top of the stairs, Ted said, "Hand that stuff up to me, Frank. Then I'll get you a beer."

"Music to my ears."

Earlier that day, Ted had cleared space in his bedroom for Marci and Frank. When Frank stepped inside, Ted said, "You and Marci can take my bedroom."

"No, Ted. We don't want to put you out."

"It's fine. I'll take the pullout couch. It's comfortable, just a little smaller." Ted hadn't actually tested the sleep sofa but wanted to put Frank at ease. "The boys can sleep in the bunk over the driver's console. It's a good thing you brought sleeping bags and pillows. I didn't think about extra sheets or blankets for the bunk. You ready for a beer?" Ted asked Frank.

"Beyond ready."

After they distributed the suitcases, pillows, and blankets, Ted said, "I hope you don't mind trying a local brew. It's pretty good."

"Sounds great."

The boys had settled on a television program and showed no intention of moving from the recliners.

Ted and Frank joined Summer and Marci chatting outside by the fire.

Summer acknowledged them with a nod, then stood and said, "I'll let you visit. Enjoy this beautiful night."

"Please, don't leave on our account," Marci said.

"I'm an early riser, which means my carriage turns into a pumpkin about this time. It was very nice to meet you both," she replied, looking first to Marci then Frank. Then she turned to Ted and smiled. "Goodnight, Teddy."

"Goodnight," the three said in unison.

They watched as Summer returned to her camper. Then Marci turned to her father and asked, "Teddy?"

Ted rolled his eyes. "I can't get her to stop calling me that."

"Is she the ditz you told me about?" Marci asked.

"I was wrong to say that. She's not a ditz. She's . . . free spirited, I guess you could say. But she's very nice."

"Yes, she seems to be . . . , Teddy." Marci smiled.

Ted dropped his chin in surrender and shook his head. "I'll never live this down, will I!"

"Never! Oh, before I forget. Dan asked me to give you this."

Marci pulled a package out of the oversized purse that sat next to her chair.

"What is it?" Ted asked.

"I don't know. Open it."

Ted tore the plain brown wrapper on the box.

"It's a blood pressure monitor." Ted saw a note stuck to the box. He read it aloud. "Twice a day, keep track. I'll call you."

"He wasn't happy you left without saying anything," Marci said.

"As I recall, none of this was my idea," Ted reminded her.

"I'm just saying you could have gone about it in a more reasonable manner."

"Wow, maybe we all do become our parents. You sound just like your mother."

"I'll take that as a compliment," Marci smiled.

Ted gazed at his daughter and smiled back. Then, happy to steer the conversation away from himself, he turned to Frank and said, "Frank, tell me what's going on in the marketing world."

The evening progressed with casual conversation until Marci said, "I can't keep my eyes open any longer. I'm going to bed."

"That sounds like a good idea," Ted said. "You two go ahead. I'll put out the fire."

Frank was lifting Casey into the bunk when Ted came through the door. "I have a ladder for that. It's in that cabinet." He pointed to a tall door behind the driver's seat, then retrieved the ladder from it and leaned it against the bunk.

"I don't think he even woke up," Frank said as he moved Casey to the far side of the bunk. "Come on, Frankie. Your turn."

Bleary eyed, Frankie Jr. climbed the ladder and crawled onto the bunk. Frank covered the boys with a sleeping bag. "Goodnight."

He received a groan in return.

Marci came out of the bedroom dressed in a bathrobe and slippers. She kissed Ted on the cheek, "Goodnight, Dad."

"Goodnight, sweetheart." Then he turned to Frank. "Goodnight."

"Do you want help with the sofa bed?" Frank asked.

"No, I've got it, thanks."

"Well, then. Goodnight, Ted."

Ted made up the sofa bed, turned out the lights, stripped to his boxers, and got under the covers. At that moment, he felt unusually happy.

⤙ ⤚

It was no surprise that Ted woke first. He had just finished getting dressed when the boys rose and, still wearing their clothes from the night before, climbed down the ladder.

"So, how did you both sleep?" Ted asked.

"Casey kept kicking me," Frankie Jr. said.

"Uh uh. You kept kicking me," Casey said, swinging his foot toward Frankie's leg. But his brother quickly pulled his leg away, causing Casey to miss and stumble.

"I meant, was the bunk comfortable?" Ted asked.

"Yeah, it was neat," Casey said. "I like it."

Frankie Jr. just nodded.

"Why don't you grab your coats. We'll go outside so we don't wake your mom and dad," Ted said.

"Our coats are in the car," Frankie Jr. replied.

The three quietly left the camper and closed the door. The morning air held a chill. Frankie Jr. and Casey joined Ted next to the firepit after retrieving their coats.

"Have you ever built a fire?" Ted asked the boys.

"We're not allowed to play with matches," Casey replied.

"That's a good rule," Ted said. "But do you know how to set up the wood for a fire?"

97

Casey shrugged his shoulders while Frankie Jr. said, "I've seen Dad do it a couple times. He makes it like a teepee."

"That's how I do it, too. Would you both like to help me?"

"Yeah!" Casey said with a wide grin.

"Sure." Frankie Jr. replied.

"Okay. Go grab a few pieces of wood," Ted directed, waving his hand toward the wood pile.

As the boys brought the logs over, Ted laid the foundation of the fire with paper and kindling. Then he demonstrated how to lean the logs against each other, placing them over the top of the kindling while explaining the need for air to flow between them. With the tepee fully constructed, he said, "Okay, stand back," and using a long handled lighter, lit the paper under the kindling. The three watched intently as the kindling caught fire first. After a short time, flames reached the dry logs, and soon, the campfire roared.

They huddled around the firepit. Ted glanced across the lane toward Summer's trailer, and a thought occurred to him. He looked at his watch. *Oh, boy. Summer is going to be taking her shower soon.*

"So," Ted said, trying to make conversation, "How's school?" *Ugh, you idiot. Kids hate school. You should never ask about school.*

"I can't wait 'til it's over. I'm going to try out for the summer league baseball team next week," Frankie said, swinging his arms as if holding a bat. "I'll make the team easy. I was the best player in little league last year."

"You know, Frankie, now that you're in junior high school, you'll be playing against kids older than you. The competition is going to be much tougher," Ted said.

Frankie's eyes widened.

"What do you mean?" Casey asked.

"I mean, in sports, or anything we do, things get harder as we get older. You don't want to be overconfident, that's all. You want to stay humble."

"What does humble mean?" Casey squinched his eyes.

"It means you don't want to assume you are better than anyone else at what you do. Whether it's sports or being a lawyer, like me."

"But Frankie is the best ballplayer around," Casey replied.

"I'm sure he is, and he might be the best in the Summer league, too. I'm just saying none of us should assume we'll get what we want. We always need to work for it." Ted glanced at Frankie Jr. "Do you understand what I'm trying to say, Frankie?"

"Yeah, I think so."

"You just do your best and listen to the coaches," Ted smiled, "and you'll do just fine."

"Sure thing, Grandpa," Frankie Jr. replied. Then he spread his legs as if standing in the batter's box and practiced his stance.

"Looking good," Ted smiled.

Frankie Jr. swung his imaginary bat at the imaginary incoming pitch.

Just then, Summer's door opened and she stepped out wearing a kimono that seemed to cover her completely. She saw them at the firepit and waved. All three waved back.

"What's she doing, Grandpa?" Casey asked.

"Do you see that green tent she's getting into?"

"Yeah," Casey said.

"That's her shower," Ted said.

The boys' eyes and mouths shot open. They watched as, moments later, steam began to rise from the tent.

"You mean, she's naked in there?" Frankie Jr. asked.

"Well, you wouldn't take a shower with your clothes on, would you?" Ted smirked.

Casey placed his hand over his mouth and began giggling. Ted could see that Frankie Jr. tried to hold back a smile, although his mouth slightly curled up on both sides.

Neither boy took his eyes off the tent. Ten minutes later, the steam stopped, and Frankie glanced toward Ted, the tip of his tongue lying on his curled bottom lip. Ted found it difficult not to chuckle.

"Is she coming out, Grandpa?" Casey asked.

"She's not going to stay in there forever," Frankie Jr. said, eyes glued to the tent.

Ted concealed a grin. "Yes, Casey. She'll come out soon. But it's not polite to stare."

If concentration paid off in dimes, the boys would have had full pockets.

Summer emerged from the tent wrapped securely in her kimono and wearing a towel on her head. Ted heard her chuckle when she looked toward them and saw where the boys' attention was focused. The boys didn't move until she entered her trailer and closed the door.

Casey turned to Ted and asked, "Grandpa, do you have a shower like that?"

"No, Casey, I have an indoor shower."

"Good, 'cuz I don't think Mom would want to do that," Casey said.

"No, I don't think she would either," Ted replied. "Why don't you throw another log on the fire, Frankie."

"Okay, Grandpa, I will . . . in a minute," Frankie said as he shifted in his chair and placed his hands on his lap.

Ted grinned. *Ah, to be thirteen again,* he thought.

Twenty minutes later, Summer reappeared fully dressed and holding a large mixing bowl and wire whisk. She opened the back doors of her van. Ted had a feeling she had a surprise in store for them.

"Does anyone over there like chocolate chip pancakes?" Summer asked, just loud enough to be heard from fifteen yards away.

The boys looked at Ted with anticipation.

"Can we, Grandpa?" Casey asked.

"Only if you use your manners," Ted replied.

The boys ran over to Summer's site. Ted followed, walking briskly.

"Why don't you boys sit at the picnic table," Ted suggested.

Frankie Jr. and Casey sat sideways, straddling the picnic table bench. Each studied the outdoor shower.

Ted stood by Summer's side. "I figured when I saw the big bowl you had something up your kimono sleeve."

"It's not very often I get to cook for two growing boys," Summer smiled.

"Boys?" Ted said, trying to divert their attention. "This is Summer. Summer, this is Frankie Jr., and this is Casey," Ted offered pointing to each respectively.

"Summer? That's your name?" Casey asked.

"Yes, it is. My mother loved the summer season and wanted to name me for something she loved," Summer explained.

"So," Casey asked, "is your last name Season?"

Summer let out a hoot. "No, but that would have made sense, wouldn't it?"

"Her last name is Case," Ted interjected.

"Actually, that's not correct," Summer said.

Ted squinted and his head slightly tilted.

"My name is Just Summer."

"Just Summer? No last name?" Frankie asked. "Like, Zendaya?"

"I'm not sure who that is but, no, not exactly. You see when I was born, my mother wanted to give me just one name, Summer. She wanted me to pick my own last name one day if I wanted one. When she told the hospital staff that my name was only Summer, they argued with her. Finally, she got so mad, she yelled at the woman filling out the paperwork and said, "Her name is Just Summer." So the woman who filled out my birth certificate wrote that my first name was Just and my last name was Summer."

"Whoa, cool," Frankie said.

"She's pulling your leg, boys," Ted said.

"The heck I am," Summer said, then went into her trailer to retrieve her driver's license. She handed it to Ted.

"Well, I'll be a son of a gun," Ted said, reading her name on the driver's license. "Just Summer."

To the boys, she said, "But you can call me Summer," then turned to Ted and relished his surprise.

"You didn't change your name when you got married?" Ted asked.

"No. I figured my mother went to great lengths to give me this name, and I wanted to honor that. So, I never changed it. Arnold knew the story well before we got married and was fine with my decision."

From the corner of his eye, Ted saw Frankie Jr. lean and whisper into Casey's ear.

"Summer?" Casey then asked.

Summer spun around. "Yes, Casey."

"Can I look in your shower?"

"Of course. Have at it." Summer smiled widely. "You can use it later if you want," she added.

The boys raced to the tent and peeked inside.

Along with the snickering, Ted heard a few whispered words— wet and soapy among them. But the word naked was uttered more than once. Ted eyed Summer with a raised brow. "They won't forget this any time soon."

Summer chuckled at Ted's assumption.

Ted's worries about interacting with his grandsons disappeared as they ate chocolate chip pancakes. By the time Marci and Frank joined them, the boys had finished their breakfast.

"Good morning, Summer, Dad. What do we have here?" Marci asked.

"Good morning," Ted replied.

"Good morning, Marci, Frank. I hope you don't mind. I haven't had the chance to cook for kids in ages," Summer replied.

"Mind? Letting us sleep in while someone else does all the work? We don't mind a bit, do we honey?" Frank asked as he smiled and put his arm around Marci's waist.

"Not at all. Whatever you made, it sure smells delicious," Marci said.

"Pancakes. Chocolate chip pancakes," Casey grinned.

"Well, I hope you thanked Summer for your breakfast," Marci said.

"We did, didn't we, Summer?" Casey asked.

"Yes, you sure did," she replied.

"We saved you some plain pancakes. The boys and I ate all the chocolate chip ones," Ted grinned.

"Sounds perfect, thank you," Marci said as she and Frank took a seat at the picnic table.

"Mom?" Casey asked.

"Yes, Casey?"

"Can I take a shower after breakfast?" he asked, as serious as a church mouse on Sunday.

Ted, Summer, and Frankie Jr. broke out in laughter.

While Marci and Frank ate their moist and fluffy pancakes, Ted asked the boys, "What do you think about boats?"

"I love boats," Frankie replied.

"Me, too," Casey concurred.

After a short disagreement between the boys on whether Casey had ever been on a boat, Marci, Frank, and Ted agreed that a boat tour on Cayuga Lake would be fun.

"Would you like to join us, Summer?" Marci asked.

"Oh, thank you, no. I have some things to do this afternoon. But I hope you have a wonderful time."

After cleaning up the breakfast dishes, they said their goodbyes to Summer and returned to Ted's camper to prepare for the outing.

An hour later, they were on the road. When they arrived at the marina, Ted purchased a set of binoculars from the gift shop. Then they boarded the boat.

TRASH TALK

TED

Standing against the railing on the port side of the boat, they heard a woman's voice through the mounted speakers.

"Hello, ladies and gentlemen. Welcome aboard the MV *Osprey*. My name is Julia, and I will be your informational tour guide for the next ninety minutes as we cruise Cayuga Lake." Julia explained safety precautions, the general layout for seating on the boat, and the location of the snack bar and two restrooms. The boat pulled away from the dock.

"What does MV stand for, Grandpa?" Frankie Jr. asked.

"It stands for motor vessel. Years ago, most boats ran on steam, so they used the letters, SS before their names, meaning steamship. But now, most boats use motors."

"The lake is home to the osprey," Julia continued, "the only hawk that survives almost entirely on fish. If you look closely, you will see nesting areas all along the lake. For those of you who don't have binoculars, you may purchase a pair in the main cabin."

"Cool," Frankie said. "Can I use the binoculars, Grandpa?"

"You and Casey will have to share," Ted replied, handing the binoculars to Frankie Jr.

Julia went on. "The osprey typically weighs about four and a half pounds and has a wingspan of approximately six feet. They're able to see their prey underwater as they soar overhead. If you spot them momentarily hovering, keep watching. It usually means they have located a fish and will suddenly dive feet first into the water. They rarely miss. Once they have a fish secured in their talons, they will find a nearby perch to feast."

Fifteen minutes later, Casey yelled, "Look, look, there's one!"

"Good job, Casey," Frank said. "Watch him, now. Let's see if he finds a fish."

The boys and Frank leaned against the boat rail and watched as the osprey searched for food.

Still standing with the others at the railing, Ted said, "What do you say we take a seat, Marci."

Marci wrapped her arm around her father's, and they sat on the outside molded plastic bench behind Frank and the boys.

"They're great kids, Marci. You and Frank have done a wonderful job."

Marci smiled. "Thanks, Dad. I'm glad you're getting a chance to spend time with them."

"Me, too," Ted replied.

"Dad?" Marci voiced quietly. "What is . . . never mind."

"What?"

"Nothing. I was just . . . I don't know. Just wondering something."

"Well, what are you wondering?"

"It's none of my business, but . . . "

"Uh, oh, are you going to grill me on my eating habits again?"

"No, that's the thing. You seem to be doing great. I wondered if maybe Summer has something to do with that?"

"Absolutely. She's a fantastic cook."

"No, I didn't mean her cooking. I noticed how well you two get along."

Ted chuckled. "Yes, we had a bit of a rough start, but she's a very nice person."

"So?" Marci asked with a sideways glance.

"So, what?"

"Are you really going to make me say it?"

"Say what? I have no idea what you're getting at."

"Could you and Summer become more than friends?" Marci spurted.

"What?" The question took Ted by surprise as the idea seemed impossible to him. "I can't believe you just asked me that."

"Why not? You said yourself that she is a nice person, and you get along so well."

"Marci, I loved your mother very much."

"I know you did. And she loved you. But she's been gone for five years. Which means you've been alone for five years. I just think . . . "

"Don't think." Ted cut her off abruptly.

Ted knew at once his response was too harsh as he saw the pained look on Marci's face.

"I'm sorry, I didn't mean to . . . Honey, there are a lot of nice people in this world, but there was only one of your mother, and I was lucky she chose me."

"But don't you . . ."

"Marci, like you said, it's none of your business. I love you, pumpkin, and I don't mean to be dismissive, but you just can't understand. And I hope to God you never will."

With sorrowful eyes, Marci placed her hand on top of her father's.

"Whoa, did you see that?" Frankie Jr. hollered.

"I saw it, I saw it," Casey screamed excitedly.

Casey ran to Marci. "Mom, did you see it? It dove right into the water and came out with a fish. Then it flew away. Grandpa, did you see it?"

"Darn, I missed it. Let me know if you see another one," Ted said.

"Okay, I will," Casey said as he strutted back to the boat rail.

"I didn't mean to pry," Marci said. "I just worry about you."

"I know, but it's not your job to worry about me. I'm doing fine. You just take care of these great kids."

After the boat tour, Ted brought them to Taughannock State Park. They waded in the pool at Lower Falls before hiking to Taughannock Falls.

Ted, Marci, and Frank leisurely walked the dirt trail that followed along the river while the boys darted in and out of the wooded area through patches of wildflowers. As they got nearer their destination, Casey asked, "What's that noise?"

Ted grinned and replied, "It's getting loud, isn't it? There's a waterfall up ahead. That's what you hear."

"It doesn't sound like water," Frankie Jr. said. "It sounds like thunder."

"It does, doesn't it?" Marci said.

They got a full view of the waterfall as they rounded a bend in the path. Casey covered his ears as the sound of water crashed into the river from above. The basin filled with mist. When the breeze shifted, crisp, clean vapor enveloped them.

Pointing to the V-shape in the cliff above that water flowed from, Ted asked the boys, "Do you see where the water has cut through the rocks?"

Frankie Jr. nodded, but Casey replied, "Water doesn't cut things, Grandpa."

"Well, technically, you are correct, Casey. It didn't really cut the rocks. It eroded them. Do you know what that means?" Ted asked Casey.

Casey squinted and pursed his lips.

"How about you Frankie? Do you know what it means?" Ted asked.

"Yeah, we learned about it in science class. The running water wears down the rocks, especially the softer rocks. That's why when you find rocks in a river, they're smooth."

"Give the man a silver dollar. You are correct," Ted pointed to Frankie and smiled.

"I don't get it," Casey said.

"Go look at the pictures on that kiosk over there. It shows you what Frankie was saying," Ted said.

The boys started to walk to the kiosk when Frankie Jr. stopped and turned. "What about the silver dollar?"

Ted laughed, reached into his pocket, and pulled out a dollar bill.

"Well, it's not silver, but it's a dollar."

Frankie ran to him and, with a great big smile, grabbed the bill from Ted's hand.

"Thanks, Grandpa," he said before running off.

Ted turned to Marci and Frank and said, "I guess I better be careful what I say around that one."

They ate dinner at a local family-friendly restaurant and finished the day with a round of miniature golf. It was eight o'clock when they returned to the campground.

"I'll make a fire," Frank said.

Frankie Jr. and Casey wouldn't admit it, but they were exhausted. They insisted on watching television before they went to bed. Within minutes, both fell sound asleep in the reclining chairs.

"I'm going to open a bottle of wine. Can I get you a beer, Frank?" Ted asked, knowing that Frank did not like wine.

"I won't say no, Ted."

"Marci, would you like some wine?"

"Absolutely," she said as she collapsed into one of the canvas folding chairs they had brought from home.

When Ted returned with the wine and beer, he said, "I'm thinking of getting some real outdoor furniture. What do you think?"

"Where would you keep it when you're not using it?" Frank asked.

"There's plenty of storage underneath the camper for a nice set of folding chairs and table," Ted answered.

"I guess that answers the question I've been wanting to ask," Marci said.

"What question is that?"

"If you're enjoying this camping thing."

"I am. Once I got settled in. I should have prepared better, but I'm getting the hang of it."

Across the way, Summer came out of her camper carrying a large plastic garbage bag. As she walked by her van, she seemed to struggle with its weight.

"Excuse me for a minute," Ted said to Marci and Frank. "Hang on, Summer," Ted called to her. "That looks heavy. Let me help you with that."

"It is. Thank you, Teddy. How was your day with the boys?" Summer asked as he approached. She set the bag on the ground.

"We had a great time. They really are good kids. We took a boat ride on the lake and played mini golf. I can't believe how grown up they are. How did dinner go?"

"There's this traveling salesman named Harry. I met him the first night I arrived here, but he left before you came. He came back today, and he brought me some fresh artichokes. He'd never eaten one before, so I steamed them and made a dipping sauce, and before I could stop him, instead of scraping the meat off the petal, he tossed a whole thing in his mouth and started chewing. You should have seen the look on his face just before he spit it out on the ground." Summer laughed. "I saved one for you."

Ted smiled. "Would you like to join us by the fire?"

"No, thank you, Teddy. I'm beat. Besides, you should spend time alone with your family. But thank you for asking."

"Goodnight." Ted said.

"Goodnight."

Ted picked up the garbage bag, walked to the dumpster, and tossed it inside.

Upon returning to the campfire, Ted continued their conversation as if he had never left.

"I was thinking of something a bit more comfortable than these canvas chairs, something sturdier."

The inquisitive look on Marci's face made Ted pause.

"What?" Ted asked.

Marci glanced at Frank who shrugged his shoulders.

"Nothing," Marci replied. "I think you should do," she hesitated, "whatever makes you happy."

Exhausted from the day's activities, they turned in early that evening.

⌒⌒ ⌒⌒

When Ted woke the next morning, he noticed Casey was alone in the bunk, still sleeping. Marci and Frank were also still sleeping. Wondering where Frankie Jr. was, Ted peeked out the window and saw him sitting by the ash-filled firepit, staring at Summer's trailer.

Ted grinned, got dressed, and joined Frankie.

"What do you say we make a fire?" Ted asked.

"All right, Grandpa," Frankie replied.

"Why don't you see if you can do it without my help," Ted said.

"Really?"

"Yes. You saw how it's done. Give it your best shot."

An excited grin spread across Frankie's face. He eagerly gathered twigs and pinecones from the ground and set them in a pile next to the firepit. Then, from the box Ted had stored under the back of the camper, he collected paper and arranged it in the pit. He topped the paper with twigs and cones, then leaned the logs over the top to form a teepee.

Ted retrieved the long-handled lighter from the storage compartment and handed it to Frankie. Then Ted heard Summer's door open and watched as, without lifting his head, Frankie diverted his eyes to her. Clearly, Ted got that Frankie did not wish to be seen as interested.

Summer emerged from her camper in her kimono and carrying a towel. Wanting to give Frankie some privacy, Ted said, "I'm going to get a glass of orange juice. Do you want one?"

"Uh uh," Frankie shook his head without shifting his glance.

Ted walked into the camper, closed the door, and headed for the window. He felt deep compassion for the boy. He remembered his own feelings at that age: the confusion, self-consciousness, and fear of anyone discovering his innermost thoughts. He recalled his father's reaction when his mother discovered a tattered *Playboy* magazine in Ted's bedroom. Afraid he would be punished, Ted was stunned when his father later returned to his bedroom with a stack of similarly worn magazines and dropped them on his bed. He remembered with disgust that it was the only time his father looked at him with pride.

"Poor kid," Ted said.

"What poor kid?" Marci asked as she came out of the bedroom.

Surprised by her presence, Ted jerked his head in her direction.

"Frankie. All I can say is I would not want to go through puberty again."

Clearly alarmed by what Ted might be seeing, Marci rushed to the window.

"Summer is in the shower," Ted explained.

"Oh," Marci said. "Isn't it too soon for this stage?"

"Absolutely not," Ted replied.

"Oh, boy."

Ted chuckled.

"I'm not ready for this."

"No parent is ever ready."

Ted kissed his daughter on the forehead and went back outside.

"How's the fire coming?" he asked.

"Huh? Oh."

Frankie turned back to the firepit. He ignited the lighter and touched the flame to the paper in four places. Fire from paper and cardboard then lit the kindling. Before long, the logs were ablaze. The fire roared, although Ted could tell that Frankie felt warm enough without it.

It wasn't until Summer had finished her shower and gone back into her camper that Ted had Frankie's full attention.

"So, Frankie, are you dating anyone back home?" Ted asked.

"Huh? No," he replied, blushing with wide eyes.

"No? Well, I imagine that will happen soon enough. You're only thirteen. No need to hurry things, right?"

Frankie eyed Ted as if trying to decide if he could trust him. Then Frankie cleared his throat and said, "There is this one girl. Her name is Carol. My friend Tommy said her friend Kimmy told him that Carol likes me."

"Carol, huh? Well, Frankie, if she's anything like your Grandma Carol, you better scoop her up before somebody else does."

Frankie smiled. "I forgot Grandma's name was Carol."

Ted nodded.

Hesitantly, Frankie asked, "Do you miss her, Grandpa?"

"Every day."

"Mom does, too. She talks about her a lot."

"I'm happy she talks about Grandma," Ted said. "So, tell me about your Carol."

Frankie laughed, "She's not my Carol. But she is smart and pretty."

"Have you talked to her?" Ted asked.

"No way."

"Why not?"

"What would I say?"

"You could start with saying hello."

"Sure, but then what?"

"Frankie, do you want to know a secret about girls?" Ted asked in a whisper.

Frankie leaned in and quietly replied, "Yeah."

"They are just people, too. You don't have to talk to them any differently than you do to anyone else. Just be nice and use your manners, like you did with Summer yesterday."

Frankie casually leaned back in his chair. "I don't know. They sure seem different."

Ted chuckled.

Just then, Marci stepped out of the trailer with Casey following.

"Where's Frank? Still sleeping?" Ted asked.

"He's taking a shower. What a perfect fire, Dad," Marci said.

"Frankie built it," Ted replied.

Frankie's face filled with pride.

"Well, I'll be a son of a duck," Marci said.

When Frank joined them, Casey blurted, "Frankie made the fire, Dad."

Standing tall with a gleam in his eyes, Frank looked at Frankie Jr. and said, "Well, I'd say this is just about one of the best campfires I've ever seen. Good job, son."

"Thanks," Frankie Jr. grinned.

They enjoyed a relaxing morning. Frankie Jr. looked proud and occasionally glanced toward Summer's trailer. Casey talked almost non-stop, shifting subjects as quickly as a hummingbird flits from one place to another. When they could get a word in, Frank and Marci discussed plans for renovating their home, and Ted just sat and listened to it all, feeling happy and at home.

By early afternoon, the van was packed, and the boys were buckled in in the back seat.

Standing beside the car, Marci asked Ted, "We'll see you at home?"

"I guess. I'm just not sure when. I don't know what my plans are," Ted replied.

"Wait, don't leave," Summer yelled from across the street. She ran toward them holding a paper plate full of brownies. "I made these for your ride home." She handed the plate to Marci.

With her free arm, Marci gave Summer a hug. "Thank you, Summer. It was great to meet you."

Frank walked from the other side of the car. "Goodbye, Summer. Thank you for breakfast and the brownies."

Summer replied, "They will cost you a hug." After they hugged, she said, "Goodbye, Frank. Goodbye, boys." Summer waved to the boys and went back to her trailer.

"She's sweet, Dad," Marci said.

"Yes, she is."

"And I know how you feel, but she's crazy about you," Marci added.

Ted chuckled. "No, Marci, it's not like that, I told you we're just friends."

"Maybe it's not like that for you," Marci said as she looked down at the plate of brownies.

Ted's Adam's apple took a deep dive down his throat, then slowly rose again.

"But we're just friends . . . I didn't do . . . we aren't."

"Dad, you took her trash out last night," Marci grinned. "I heard what you said about Mom being the only one for you, but maybe you should keep an open mind. I'll call you when we get home. I love you." She reached up and kissed Ted on the cheek.

Ted shook Frank's hand and waved goodbye to the boys before they pulled away.

Alarmed by Marci's assertion that Summer had feelings for him, Ted glanced toward her campsite. Summer was outside tidying up. She saw him looking over and shot him a quick wave and smile. In panic, Ted turned and closed himself in his trailer.

Racked with guilt, Ted tried to recall if he had done anything to give Summer the wrong impression. Marci's comment about taking out her trash only served to confuse him. *Apparently,* he thought, *any little gesture could have been taken the wrong way.* Aside from guilt, he felt panic and anxiety. It thrust him back to his early teens when he didn't know how to act around or talk to girls.

His father's idea of wooing a woman was to whistle at her and grab her butt. When Ted tried that approach at the age of thirteen, the girl whose butt that he touched poured a super-sized cola on his head.

With each thought, Ted became less confident about socializing with Summer, and that made him sad. *Maybe it's time to go home*, Ted thought.

Midafternoon on the second full day of Ted's self-imposed seclusion, Summer knocked on his door. Ted pretended to be asleep until she went away.

He knew he couldn't hide forever. If he hadn't paid for the campsite for the month, he would have just packed up and left. But his father's voice kept telling him, *You paid for this and made the commitment. You have to stick it out. Money doesn't grow on trees, you know.* Besides, he knew running away wouldn't be right.

UH OH

SUMMER

After not seeing Ted for two days, Summer began to think the worst. She pictured him lying on the floor of his camper and unable to call for help. As much as she tried to think of plausible reasons for Ted's seclusion, she could think of none.

On the third morning, Summer approached the campground owners and asked that they do a wellness check on Ted. She followed them to Ted's door.

"Mr. Winter, this is Candace Hartley, the campground owner," she said loudly as she knocked on his door. "Mr. Winter, are you in there?"

Ted opened the door. Candace, her husband, and Summer stood at the bottom of the stairs.

Summer quietly gasped when she saw him. He hadn't shaved or combed his hair and, at 10 a.m., he was still in his bathrobe.

"Yes? What can I do for you?" Ted asked.

"Teddy, are you all right?" Summer asked.

With only a quick glance toward Summer, Ted's gaze shifted toward Candace and her husband, and he said, "I'm fine. What's this about?"

"Miss Summer asked us to check on you. She was worried," Candace answered.

He addressed Candace. "Well, as you can see, I am fine. Thank you for your concern. I'm sorry if I worried you."

"Oh, it's no trouble at all. Sorry to have bothered you," Candace said.

Ted nodded as he shut his door.

"Thank goodness, everything seems to be fine," Candace said to Summer as she and her husband turned to leave.

"Yes . . . fine. Thank you," Summer responded, while thinking, *No, he's not fine. Something is wrong.*

Summer stayed behind. "Teddy? What's going on?" she yelled toward the door. "Teddy?"

Clearly annoyed at Summer's persistence, Ted opened the door. The fact that he barely looked at her did not escape her notice. "What is it?"

"I'm worried about you," Summer said.

"There's no need to worry. I'm fine. But I'm busy right now."

"Are you angry with me, Teddy?"

"I've asked you a hundred times not to call mc that!"

Summer took a step back. *He is angry at me. What did I do?* "All right, Ted. I'm sorry. Did I do something wrong? Did I overstep when your daughter was here?"

"I think you assume too much, Summer. I don't think I can deal with that. I told you, I'm not good at this kind of thing. Now, if you'll excuse me . . . ," Ted said before he shut the door.

Staggered as at the instant an arrow hits a doe's heart, Summer stood swaying before her metaphorical drop to the ground.

She just didn't understand. She replayed the weekend over and over in her mind. The only thing she could imagine was that she intruded on Ted's family time when she made breakfast for the boys. *And then I gave them brownies,* she thought. *Is that it? Does he think I was trying to outshine him?*

Summer walked slowly back to her camper. She thought she had finally made a close friend, someone her own age to talk to, to enjoy a glass of wine with. Someone who understood the pain of loss, like she did. She thought he felt the same. And then, without any reason she could understand, it seemed he didn't wish to be friends at all. *Have I been that wrong?*

How can I be sure about anything if I can be this wrong about a person?

Summer sat in her camper and did something she hadn't done in years. She cried. A full body-shaking, breathless, headache-producing cry. Not since Arnold died had she cried so intensely. Losing both her parents hadn't made her cry so deeply.

What does that say about me? she wondered. *What does it say about my soul?*

TED

Ted felt sick to his stomach. He had seen the hurt in Summer's eyes, and it was entirely his fault. *Did I mislead her? Did I make her think I could ever be with anyone but Carol?* He thought she understood they were just friends.

And we are friends, he thought. *Were.* He had enjoyed spending time with her. It was nice having someone his own age to talk to. Someone who had lived through similar circumstances. And she was one of the most honest people he had ever met.

I am a horrible person. She's better off without me.

Three days passed before Ted ran into Summer at the camp store.

"Hello, Ted," Summer politely said.

"Hello, Summer," Ted returned in kind.

Then both went about their separate ways.

A few nights later, each made a campfire. Ted saw that Summer had already settled beside her firepit, seated facing Ted's camper. Ted decided to sit with his back towards Summer to avoid awkward eye contact.

Ted's phone rang.

"Hello, Marci," Ted said in a soft voice.

"Hi, Dad. Why are you whispering?" Marci asked.

Ted got out of his chair and moved inside the camper. "I'm not whispering. How are you? How are the boys and Frank?"

"We're good. Frankie Jr. wants to talk to you. Here he is."

"Hey, Grandpa," Frankie said.

"Hey, Frankie, how are you?"

"I'm great, Grandpa. I made the baseball team. They said they are going to start me at shortstop."

"Congratulations, kid. Good for you. I'm proud of you."

"I did like you said. I listened to the coaches and did everything they said. It's a good thing, too, because some of the kids didn't, and they didn't make the team. Even though they were good ballplayers. I just wanted to tell you that."

Ted choked up. He was proud of Frankie and happy that his advice may have had some impact on Frankie's success. "Well, thank you, Frankie. But this was all you. You did this on your own. You should be proud."

"Yeah, I am. Thanks, Grandpa," he said sincerely. "Gotta go. Mom wants to talk to you."

"Bye, Frankie."

"So, Dad, how's everything going?" Marci asked.

"Fine," he responded, trying to sound upbeat.

"How's Summer?"

"I imagine she's all right."

"What do you mean, you imagine? Did she leave?"

"No, she's still here."

"You don't see her every day?" Marci asked.

"No. I don't see her every day," Ted said wearily.

"What's going on? Did you two have a fight or something?"

"Of course not. We just each have our own lives."

"You're being vague. When is the last time you talked to her?"

"I'm not being vague. If you want to know what's going on with Summer, call Summer."

"I would, but I don't have her number. Tell me what's going on."

"Look, we just don't talk much anymore, that's all." Ted sighed. He didn't want to elaborate on his current relationship with Summer, but Marci would not let up.

"Why?"

"Because I don't want her to think I'm looking for what she's looking for."

Marci's volume rose, and she rushed her words. "Have you talked to Summer since we were there?"

"Not really, no. A couple times, maybe. I may have said a few things."

"Oh, no. What did you say?"

"Does it really matter, sweetheart."

"Yes, it does. If this is my fault, it matters a lot," Marci said.

"Nothing's your fault, honey. There was nothing there to begin with. Just relax and enjoy Frankie's good news. I've got to go. I'll talk to you later."

Ted hung up. His heart was racing. He placed his hand on his chest and steadied his breathing.

It was then he made some decisions. *To hell with it. It's my money, and I'll decide how to spend it. No amount of money is worth this stress. Sorry, Dad, you lose this one.* He decided to leave the campground the next day and forfeit the remaining five days on his monthly pass. *I'm going home, but I'm not going back to work.*

He dialed his business partner's cellphone.

"Well, I lost the pool. You lasted longer than I thought you would," Chip said as soon as he picked up.

"What pool?"

"The one for how long it would take you to come back to work. I guessed it would be within ten days of the last time we talked. I can't believe it's been four weeks."

"Yea, well, things happen," Ted said then got right to the point. "Listen, Chip, I need you to draw up the papers."

"Okay, sure. Which client?"

Ted hesitated. "Me," he finally said. "I'll be back in two days. We can sign them then."

"You? What papers? Back from where?"

"I'm in New York, but I'll be back in town on Thursday."

"Okay, but you still haven't told me what you need," Chip said. "Is everything all right? Are you okay?"

"Yes, I'm fine. I said *the* papers. It's time for me to move on, for you to take over the firm. It shouldn't take you long to draw them up. We worked out the details years ago. That is, if you still agree with that deal?"

Ted heard nothing from the other end of the phone.

"Chip? Did I lose you?"

"Ah, no, I'm here."

"Well?"

"You're kidding, right?"

"When was the last time you heard me joke about the business?" Ted asked.

"Jesus, Ted. This firm is your baby. Wait, are you really okay? Is something going on that I should know about?"

"I'm fine. I'm probably in the best shape I've been in for years. It's just time. I'm ready to back away, and you're more than ready to step forward."

"Hang on. There are other options to consider. You could keep some of your shares and work part time as a consultant or some other arrangement. You could work whenever you want, make your own schedule, and still have a say in the day-to-day business."

"No, I've been thinking about this for weeks, and I've made up my mind. You know what happens when I make up my mind."

"Yeah," Chip answered. "You become immovable unless the circumstances change. What I'm saying is the circumstances might change and I wouldn't want you to regret your decision. You worked too hard for this."

"Draw up the papers. I'll be there Thursday."

He hung up the phone, poured himself a glass of wine, and, feeling relieved, spent the remainder of his evening by the campfire.

SORRY I MISSED YOU

SUMMER

The next morning, Summer finished her breakfast and was about to wash her dishes when she heard a knock at her door.

Thinking it could only be Ted, she felt a surge of relief.

She opened the door to Candace Hartley.

"Good morning, Miss Summer. I'm sorry to bother, you but you have a phone call at the office."

"A phone call? Who is it?"

"I don't know. My husband answered it. He just sent me to tell you. He said it was important."

Summer threw a wrap around herself and followed Candace to the camp office. She glanced behind her to Ted's dark trailer as she walked. She assumed her lawyer had misplaced her number. He was the only person she could think of who knew she was staying at the campground.

The landline telephone receiver lay on the office desk.

Summer picked it up and warily said, "Hello?"

"Hello, Summer? This is Marci, Ted's daughter."

"Oh, hello, Marci. Is everything all right?"

"You tell me," Marci said. "I may have caused a horrible problem. Have you spoken to my father?"

Summer paused. "No, I haven't. Your father made it very clear that he has no interest in carrying on our friendship."

"That's what I was afraid of. This is all my fault," Marci said. "I made a terrible mistake. I was just so happy to see my father, well . . . happy."

"I don't understand. What is it you are trying to say?"

"That night we left, I told him that I thought you might be interested in him. I mean, you two seemed to be having such a nice time. It was an innocent comment, but I should have known my father would react this way. He's been so closed off since my mother died. I wasn't thinking. I'm so sorry."

Summer put her hand to her cheek and said, "Are you telling me that your father thinks I'm falling for him and is freaking out?"

"Yes, I think so," Marci said.

Summer began to chuckle, then laugh, then hoot. "Oh, thank God."

"Excuse me?" Marci said.

"Oh, Marci, I've been turning this thing around in my head for over a week now thinking I did something wrong. Either that or Ted was not the man he seemed to be, and that thought seemed worse."

"I am so sorry. I've tried to talk to him, but he's in full defense mode."

"Don't worry. I'll take care of it. Thank you for calling."

Poor Ted. He's a loyal man. I get it. I'm sure his thoughts went straight to betrayal. No wonder he pulled away. I'm going to fix this right now.

Filled with optimism, she stepped out of the office just in time to see Ted's motorhome drive out of the campground. Her heart sank. Not wanting to believe that she couldn't make things right between them, she thought, *Maybe he's just going to the store.*

But when she returned to her trailer, there was a note stuck to her door.

Sorry I missed you.
Ted

She tore the note from the door and went inside. *He was the only real friend I've made in a long time,* she thought as she slouched in her kitchenette. She had made acquaintances over the past several years, but hers and Ted's friendship had felt substantially deeper. She'd thought he had felt the same way. He'd been the first to think of her as just a person, not a chef, corporate president, caregiver, or billionaire. With him she could be Just Summer, and she'd enjoyed it immensely. His departure left her with an emptiness she thought she had shed. *All because of a misunderstanding.*

She felt sorry for Ted. And for herself, a reaction she rarely allowed and worked hard not to give in to.

Summer sat up straight and took stock of her feelings. She began to question the deep sadness that engulfed her. *Why is this hitting me so hard?*

Her right leg bobbed nervously up and down on the ball of her foot. *He was my friend. Is that it? Or was Marci right?*

Hoping to ease her restlessness, she stood. *Do I have deeper feelings for him?* She shook her head to dislodge the thoughts. *It doesn't matter. He's gone and I'm going to miss him.*

Summer glanced at the evening's dinner menu sitting on the table. *I don't want to think about this anymore. I'm going to start prepping dinner.*

The sink held dirty dishes from breakfast. She filled it with hot soapy water and scrubbed them with more purpose than usual. *This is just crazy. What would make him think I have a thing for him?* She placed a spotless saucepan in her drying rack.

Nope, I'm not going to think about Ted.

After putting away the dishes and pans, she drained and cleaned the sink. *Here I am just trying to be pleasant and helpful, and he goes off the deep end.*

She reached for the bag of apples sitting on the counter, then took a vegetable peeler from a kitchen drawer. *Of course, Marci gave him a push, but she didn't know any better.*

Peels sat piled next to the cutting board as she cored and diced apples. *I never did anything to suggest I wanted to be more than friends.*

While tossing together cranberry-apple herb stuffing, she considered, *Did I?*

She hesitated, then ran several of their interactions through her mind—sipping wine by the campfire and chatting, an innocent walk through the park, eating pancakes with his grandchildren. *No, of course not. Why would I? I'm not looking for any kind of relationship other than friendship,* she thought as she took a package of pork from her refrigerator.

As she relentlessly pounded pork cutlets with her meat mallet, she reflected, I thought we were friends. I thought I finally found someone I could talk to, the way I used to talk with Arnold. Well, maybe not exactly like Arnold. I could always be myself with him. I never had to mince words. I thought I had gotten as lucky with Teddy. Maybe there is no one else on this earth like Arnold. Maybe I'm destined to live the rest of my life with many acquaintances and no true friends.

The thought stung. As she wrapped the cutlets to store them in her fridge, she was struck by a disconcerting question. God, am I that desperate?

Summer reached for a new cutting board from the overhead cabinet and began to slice peaches for cobbler. *What if I come off that way? Am I so determined to make friends that I pushed too hard? Maybe it was my fault. But he needs to take responsibility for our friendship, too. He could have said something instead of hiding in his trailer. He could have . . .*

"Son of a duck," Summer exclaimed as she looked down at her cutting board to see she'd pulverized the peach. Frustration immediately set in when she realized she had used one of Ted's idioms. "What grown man says things like that, anyway?"

She reached for a new peach.

Summer mixed minced fruit with slices and prepared the cobbler. Setting aside the oven-ready dessert, she washed her cutting board to ready it for the parsnips.

As she reached for the vegetable peeler, her hand brushed the note Ted had left on her camper door.

"'Sorry I missed you.' What the hell is that? Is he the UPS driver?" she barked as she shed the parsnips of their skin.

Her sharp knife sliced through the root vegetable as if it were butter.

"Sorry I didn't say goodbye. Sorry I'm an inconsiderate juvenile. Sorry I was an ass," she ranted.

As she tossed the parsnip slices with oil and seasonings, she continued her outburst. "Sorry I hurt your feelings. Sorry I'm an idiot."

Summer stopped abruptly, looked down at her olive-oil-coated hands, and cried.

"You're being a fool." Summer used her forearm to wipe her eyes. *I am perfectly fine. I'm going to meet plenty of new people. Good riddance, Teddy.*

With the cobbler in the oven and trying to clear her mind of everything Ted, she picked up her book and sat outside.

Several chapters in, having had to reread multiple paragraphs due to lack of concentration, she heard the unmistakable sound of Ted's large motorhome rounding the bend.

Her heart jumped. She dropped the book and placed her hands on her chest. *What the heck was that?*

Her heated face evidenced that a rose tint had crept into her cheeks. She removed her hands from her chest and placed them on her warm cheeks. A tingle traveled from the base of her fingers to the tips as she sat and watched Ted drive down the lane and back his RV into the campsite.

Then, as quickly as her sadness had turned to scintillation, Summer suddenly felt duped. She thought he had left for good, the idea that he had returned incensed her, and her cheeks went from pink to crimson in a flash.

Stewing while waiting for Ted to exit the motorhome, she stood and marched the five yards to the edge of the lane that separated their sites. His feet barely hit the ground when Summer yelled, "What the hell are you doing here?"

"What do you mean?" Ted asked.

"It isn't a trick question. What are you doing here?"

"This is my campsite," Ted said, then double-checked the site number to make sure.

She rolled her eyes. *Of course, it's your campsite. But you left.* Then said, "I thought you left?"

"Why would you think that?"

"Because you left."

"I had to pick up a few things at the store."

"You left me a note."

"I wanted you to know that I stopped by."

"It sounded like a bad goodbye note, Ted."

"It was a 'sorry I missed you' note," Ted responded with a slight edge. "To me, that means someone stopped by and wanted to let you know they were sorry they missed you."

Summer huffed, then hesitated only a moment before she shouted, "I don't love you, Ted."

"What?" Ted screeched. By the sound of his voice and the way his eyes shot open, Summer knew she had shocked him.

"I'm not in love with you."

Ted turned to his right, then to his left, as if trying to hide but finding no cover. Seemingly exasperated, he threw his hands in the air and replied, "Okay."

"Marci called me this morning," Summer said.

Slowly shaking his head, Ted lowered his chin to his chest. When he looked up, he said, "Look, Summer, can we stop screaming across the street?"

"I can't leave. I have food in the oven."

"Okay, just let me hook up the electric and water, and I'll come over."

Summer walked back to her chair, still stewing. Whether it was because she was angry at Ted for shutting her out and making her cry or for his cryptic note, she didn't know. *Or am I mad at myself? What the hell is wrong with me? What am I feeling?*

Ted walked across the lane into her campsite and then stood next to Summer. Her heart jumped again. She felt a sense of relief.

"Uh oh," she whispered.

"Uh oh, what?" Ted asked.

"Nothing. Sit down, Ted," Summer said as she reached into her van for a bottle of bourbon.

"Summer, it's noon," Ted said, eyeing the bottle.

"If ever a conversation warranted a bottle of Jim Beam, this is it." Summer poured two glasses.

"Teddy. Excuse me. Ted," Summer struggled with his preferred name. "Marci called me this morning and informed me that you think I am falling in love with you, and that's why you've been such an ass for the last week and a half.

"Take a drink," Summer said handing him the glass. "Then it's your turn to speak."

Without touching it, Ted inched his nose to the rim and inhaled. His eyelids shot upward as he backed away from the drink. However, Summer sensed that Ted took her gesture as a personal challenge.

He took the bourbon from her and reluctantly sipped. His eyes momentarily bulged, and he coughed lightly. But when the burn on his tongue and lips subsided, he said, "My daughter told me that you were interested in being more than friends. I didn't give you any reason to think I was romantically interested in you. I'm not, and I can't be. Taking out your trash was not meant to be a romantic gesture."

It was Summer's turn for bulging eyes. "What the hell does trash have to do with romance? I don't . . . "

Ted interrupted. "Wait. Aren't you supposed to take a drink first?"

Summer took a nip of the bourbon and asked again, "What does my trash have to do with any of this?"

"Is it my turn?"

Summer nodded anxiously.

Ted took a hefty gulp. "Marci said that because of how you felt about me, taking out your trash meant more than taking out your trash."

Summer drank again. "That's the most ridiculous thing I've ever heard. I like you, Tedd—Ted. I thought we were having a nice friendly time together."

Ted slugged the bourbon, "That's what I thought, too. I'm not ready for anything else with anyone. It has nothing to do with you personally. I enjoy your company very much."

Summer swigged. "I enjoy your company, too. I don't have many close friends. I can't afford to lose one."

Ted slurped, "Neither do I. Are we good?"

They tapped their glasses together and then, with one last gulp, emptied them.

"We're good," Summer said.

"You scared the hell out of me." Ted said.

"I'm sorry," Summer replied. "But you made me cry."

"I'm sorry."

They shared a moment of silence.

"You know, my grandson has a thing for you," Ted smiled.

"I know."

TED

An hour later, his cell phone rang and woke Ted from his nap.

"Hello?"

"Ted, it's Dan."

"Oh, hey Dan."

"Are you all right? You sound a little groggy."

"Yeah. I was just sleeping off some bourbon."

"At four in the afternoon?" Dan asked sounding discouraged.

"It's a long story. What's up?"

"I was calling to check on you. Apparently, it's a good thing I did. Is this what you call taking care of yourself? Day drinking?"

"Relax. It's not like that. It was just one glass of bourbon, although she did fill it up pretty good," Ted said, cinching his forehead with his thumb and forefinger.

"She?" Dan asked. "Did you entertain a lady friend today?"

"Entertain a . . . Not you, too, Dan. Have you been talking to Marci?"

"As a matter of fact, yes. She called me a little while ago. She's worried about you, and now I understand why."

"And what is it you think you understand?"

"Well, what should I think? It sounds like you're living like a teenage boy, drinking and . . . cavorting."

Ted's chin fell heavy to his chest. "I'm not drinking and cavorting. I had one drink with a friend and then took a nap. Does that sound like a teenage boy?"

"Have you been taking your blood pressure?"

"Sort of."

"Sort of? What kind of answer is that?"

"I did when you first sent the darn thing, but I haven't lately."

"Take it now."

"Come on."

"Do you want me to send Marci to come and get you and bring you into my office? Take it now."

"All right. I have to go get it."

Ted put the phone on speaker, set it on the kitchen table, and retrieved the blood pressure monitor from the bathroom. "You're treating me like a child," he yelled from the bathroom, then returned to the table with the monitor.

"You're acting like one," Dan replied.

"You should come visit. You would like it here. There are plenty of golf courses."

"Don't talk while taking your blood pressure," Dan reprimanded.

Ted wrapped the armband just above his elbow and turned on the monitor. He took a few deep breaths then hit the start button. The armband quickly filled with air and squeezed Ted's arm until it felt uncomfortable. Then the machine beeped, flashed numbers, and the armband deflated.

Dan asked, "Well?"

"148 over 80."

"It's a little high but not too bad. What about your heartbeat? It's the number in the lower right-hand corner with the little heart next to it."

"98," Ted replied.

"Good. How are you feeling, in general?"

"I feel great. I've been walking every day and watching what I eat. I'm not giving up wine, though. They've got some pretty good wine here."

"As long as you drink in moderation, it shouldn't be a problem. No more daytime binge drinking."

"I'm not . . . never mind."

"Now, tell me about this lady friend," Dan said.

ENLIGHTENMENT

SUMMER

The smell of fall filled Summer's camper—apples and cinnamon with a dose of rosemary. As pork cutlets sizzled in the pan, Summer considered the feelings searing inside her.

She honestly didn't know what to make of them. Why had her heart fluttered when Ted came back? She didn't consciously have more than friendship in mind. But it happened twice.

She began to wonder if she and Ted had a history.

Through books she read as a young woman, Summer had come to believe in reincarnation. Every time she discussed the concept with her mother, it angered her father, and he dismissed the notion as ramblings of a crazy woman. Although her mother had not entirely bought in to the idea, she remained open-minded for as long as her mind functioned properly.

Summer trusted she had lived many lives before and, until she achieved enlightenment, she would live many more.

She also believed in soul groups—that souls come back to earth together in different incarnations to learn and grow and teach. On their first date, she knew she and Arnold were soulmates. And she assumed her parents were part of her soul group. She had learned so much from them in this lifetime. She had learned compassion, especially for emotionally flawed individuals. She learned patience and the importance of serving others. From Arnold, she learned faith, faith in her belief that someday she would be with him again.

So, if her soul group included Ted, it might make sense that she would think they had a history. *Maybe we were lovers in another lifetime*, she considered.

Her heart fluttered at the thought.

"Oh, for chrissake, stop that!" Summer screeched as she placed her hand over her heart.

I'd best not think about Teddy right now. I'm glad we cleared things up, Summer thought. But her instincts told her not everything was quite so clear.

After dinner, they had much to catch up on. Ted opened a Cabernet that neither he nor Summer had yet tried.

The bottle was nearly empty before Ted said, "I was going to leave tomorrow. That's why I wanted to talk to you earlier. That's why I left the note. I just didn't know what to say."

"Oh, I see. Do you still plan on leaving?" Summer asked.

"No."

"I'm glad."

"Me, too, if for no other reason than you haven't told me what you think the meaning of life is yet."

"That's right, I haven't. But, seeing that you're a flight risk, I think I'll wait a little longer before I do."

Ted chuckled. "Well, I imagine learning the secret to the meaning of life is worth waiting for. But I am going to have to leave next week, at least for a few days."

"Something important?"

"I'm officially retiring. I'm selling my shares of the firm to my business partner."

"That's a big step, Ted. Are you sure you've thought this through? Your partner isn't some sort of robber bee, is he?"

"What's a robber bee?"

"A robber bee scouts bee colonies, then steals honey from them to bring back to their own. They reap the rewards of the hard work of others."

"No. Chip's a unique character, but he's not a robber bee."

"Well, I think it's fantastic, but I hope you are doing it for the right reason. I hope you don't feel pressured by anyone."

"You mean by Marci."

"No, I mean by anyone. This should be your decision, and your decision alone. I know a little something about that."

"Were you pressured to sell Case Candle?" Ted asked.

"From the moment Arnold passed away."

"But you held onto it for. . . what? Almost fifteen years? That couldn't have been easy."

"It wasn't. But I had a responsibility to take care of the employees. So I waited until the right deal came along at the right time and took it."

"Well, this deal has been sealed for some time. It's just a matter of a few signatures."

"As long as someone else isn't pushing your pen, I'm very happy for you."

"I've realized I enjoy waking up in the morning and listening to the birds. I want to go to Frankie's baseball games and get to know what makes Casey tick. Maybe see the Grand Canyon and Yellowstone Park. No, I'm ready. Nobody's pushing my pen."

"Well, then, this calls for a toast. To a new chapter." Summer lifted her wine glass and tapped Ted's. "Cheers."

"Cheers."

"But don't you think it's a little crazy driving that motorhome back and forth? It seems to me that your partner is the one who's making out on this deal. He should come to you."

"Hmmm, that's an interesting point. You're right. I'll call him in the morning and see if we can work it out."

"And, for the record, I would never think of Marci in a negative way. She loves you very much. You're a very fortunate man."

Ted smiled.

An easy silence followed.

Minutes passed before Ted said, "I'm thinking of getting a proper set of outdoor furniture. This is nice, but I think if I had more comfortable chairs and maybe a table to sit at during the day, I would be outside more often."

Summer grinned. "It's getting under your skin, isn't it?"

"What is?"

"Camping, nature, peace. Whatever you want to call it."

"I suppose it is. Do you know if there is a furniture store nearby?"

"Not that I've seen. At least none that would have what you're looking for. Remember, whatever you buy, you need to be able to store it in that beast." Summer flipped her hand toward the motorhome. "Why don't you order something?"

"Order? From where?"

"You have a laptop computer, right?"

"Yes."

"Find something online that you like and have it delivered."

"Delivered here? Will they do that?"

"Absolutely."

"How do you know what you're buying is good quality?"

"Read the reviews."

"Reviews?"

Summer squinted and looked at Ted. "Ted, have you never bought anything online?"

"No, I haven't. I go to the store like a normal person."

"Normal? I think your normal is about twenty years in the rearview mirror. Tomorrow, I'll show you the new norm, unfortunate as it may be."

⤝ ⤞

The following day, Ted sat at Summer's folding table with a cup of coffee and a cinnamon-swirl muffin.

"Hey, I can get a rocking chair," Ted said with enthusiasm while browsing his laptop.

Summer chuckled. "I created a monster. Just make sure you pay attention to the descriptions. And read the reviews and specs."

"Should I get lights? I like your lights. All I have is that little lantern I bought at the camp store. I'm going to get lights."

Summer just shook her head.

"This can't be right," Ted said. "It says I will get this stuff tomorrow if I order in the next three hours. How is that possible?"

"It's a big company, Ted. They have warehouses everywhere and their own fleet of delivery trucks."

"That's smart."

"I don't understand how it's possible that you never bought anything online."

"Why would I buy something online when I can go to the store and get it? Look at this. I can order the coffee I like."

"Uh huh. I'm going to get my dinner started while you go down the rabbit hole."

"Huh?" Ted said without taking his eyes off the laptop screen.

When the delivery truck arrived the next day, Summer counted nine large boxes.

Meticulously organized, Ted opened each box with a pocketknife, removed the item or items, then proceeded to cut the box into firepit-sized pieces and place the cardboard into the container he stored under his trailer for fire-starting purposes. Only then did he examine his purchase.

Summer observed from across the way with the joy of watching a young boy open birthday presents, and her heart fluttered once again.

Ted had purchased four chairs: two rocking and two standards, all with armrests and wide blue cushions. He placed the standard chairs at his new six-foot folding table. The rockers sat next to the fireplace. The process took Ted fifty-five minutes to accomplish, and he still had four boxes to open.

At that point, Summer thought she should share a handy piece of online shopping experience.

"Ted," she said as she walked across the lane to his site, "You might want to wait before you cut up the boxes in case you need to send anything back."

"I can send stuff back?"

"Yes. If you don't like it, if it's broken, or if they sent the wrong product, you can send it back. But the seller usually requires it be sent back in its original packaging."

"But I have a system."

"Excuse me?" Summer asked.

"I have a system."

"So, change your system. Open up all the packages, check to make sure you're going to keep everything, then cut up the boxes."

"But it will be a mess."

Summer inspected Ted's expression. He appeared to struggle with the concept.

She replied, "Only for a few minutes. It was just a thought. I'll go away now," Summer said as she returned to her campsite.

Summer continued to watch Ted open a box, cut the box, and store it away, then inspect the items from the package.

"What the hell is that all about?" she murmured.

Ted spent the day organizing new purchases, then hanging outdoor lights. The process became excruciating for Summer to witness. Ted used a tape measure to make sure the lightbulbs were equidistant from each other and from the ground. And then, presumably realizing that the ground he stood on was not level, eyeballed each bulb so they hung as perfectly level as possible.

Dinner had come and gone by the time Ted finished his unpacking and set up. When Summer went across the lane with a plate of food for Ted, he asked, "Well? What do you think?"

Seeing his wide smile, Summer chose her words carefully. "I think it looks perfect."

Satisfaction spread across Ted's face. "Thank you for dinner. You didn't have to do that."

"I know. But you've been working so hard over here."

"No, not really," Ted said as he placed the dinner plate on the table. "Can I get you something? Wine? Coffee? I've got plenty of coffee now."

"No, thank you, Ted. I'll leave you alone to eat your dinner. I'm going to start a fire. Come over if you feel up to it."

"I will. Thanks again," Ted said with a grin.

While building her fire, Summer kept an eye on Ted. He seemed happier than he had since she met him. *As if he were injected with endorphins*, she thought.

After he finished his dinner, she watched him stand from his chair and take several moments to arrange it, square to the table—not too far in, not too far away, and directly across from the chair on the opposite side.

"Boy, did your father do a number on you, Teddy," Summer whispered.

Ted brought Summer's cleaned dish back to her along with a steaming cup of coffee.

"No wine tonight?" Summer asked.

"No, not tonight. I'm feeling pretty good without it. The coffee is sure hitting the spot, though."

"Will it bother you if I relax with a little Mary Jane?" Summer asked as she held up her bong.

"Not at all. I used to smoke myself back in the day. I enjoyed getting a little buzz, just enough to mellow out," Ted said.

"Mellow out. There's a phrase I would have placed money on that I would never hear you say."

Ted laughed. "You don't know everything about me, you know."

"I'm beginning to understand that," Summer said. "What made you stop smoking pot?"

"My father found out."

"How old were you?"

"Twenty-two. I was in college." Ted absently rubbed his hand over his left cheek. The significance did not escape Summer.

"I've been curious. What did your father do for a living when he couldn't get into the army?"

"He was an IRS auditor."

Summer choked out a puff of smoke. "You don't say. Kind of like the drill sergeant of taxes."

"Yes, I suppose he was. I never thought of it that way."

Ted suddenly made sense to Summer. She had thought Ted's stiff demeanor an odd quirk. But now she thought it remarkable that Ted could relax at all.

The question remained. Could he honor his past but forge his own future? *Can any of us*, Summer thought.

Brought out of her thoughts, she heard Ted say, "My business partner is coming tomorrow. He's going to stay overnight. We'll get the paperwork done, and that will be that."

"That's good news. Will you bring him by for dinner?"

"Of course. I imagine he will be grateful not to eat my cooking."

"I look forward to meeting him."

"Don't get too excited. Chip is sort of . . . an acquired taste. He's a little rough around the edges and fancies himself a ladies' man. He's one heck of a lawyer, though."

"How did you come to work with him?"

"I hired him fresh out of Harvard, top of his class. I needed help, and he was hungry. He still is. I made him a partner after twelve years."

"He sounds impressive," Summer said.

"Oh," Ted laughed, "he'll leave an impression, all right."

A NEW CHAPTER

TED

The next afternoon, Chip arrived in his candy apple red Dodge Challenger. He dressed in khakis with a light pink oxford shirt topped with a Christmas red Greg Norman quarter zip sweater. His sockless feet wore loafers, and he finished the look with a red and black plaid Scally cap perched on his head.

"How was your drive?" Ted asked.

"Long and lonely. How the hell did you find this place? You're in the middle of nowhere."

"Hardly. This is wine country."

"Yeah, well, the tallest thing I've seen is the gas station sign off the highway."

They shook hands, and then Chip let out a whistle.

"Wow, this is some machine, huh? What kind of mileage does it get?"

"Oh, I don't know, I didn't pay attention. Come on. Grab your suitcase, and I'll show you the inside."

After a quick tour, Chip said, "All the comforts, huh? Where are you going to take it?"

"I haven't thought that far ahead. I like it here, so I've decided to stay for a while."

"I won't kid you. Your phone call surprised the hell out of me. I figured I'd see you in your grave before you retired."

"You almost did, remember?" Ted grinned. "I did a little kicking and screaming at first, but, well, things have changed."

"What kind of things? Is hell freezing over and I'm the last to know?"

Ted chuckled not because he thought Chip was funny but to be polite.

"No, Marci was pretty adamant after my heart attack. And the doctor presented a compelling argument. But mostly it's the grandkids. I want to get to know them, spend time with them, go to their ballgames and school activities."

"What, like plays and spelling bees?" Chip asked.

"Maybe. Why not?"

"Jesus. I know you like to keep things low-key, but that sounds torturous." Chip laughed, then paused. "But, in all seriousness, I need to know you are positive this is what you want. You've put your blood and sweat into this firm. And, just to remind you, there are other options. You could work part time or consult. Maybe hang on to the controlling shares in case you change your mind."

"No. I've made up my mind. I'm ready."

"Okay, then let's get this done so we can enjoy . . . what? What do you enjoy in a place like this?"

"Dinner!" Ted smiled.

At 5:55, when Ted and Chip had finished signing papers, the sound of the loud reverberating gong replaced the quiet.

"What the hell is that?" Chip asked.

"That's the dinner bell."

Ted stood, retrieved two plates from the kitchen cabinet, and handed one to Chip. "Follow me," he said with a sly grin.

The line had already begun to form.

"Jesus, what is this? A bread line? If you needed money, why didn't you say so?" Chip whispered.

Ted chuckled as he took a step forward in line. When they reached the front, Summer greeted them with a hearty smile.

Ted could not hold back a playful grin as he introduced them. "Chip, this is our resident chef, Summer. Summer, this is my business partner, Chip."

"It's nice to meet you, Chip."

"Likewise," Chip said, smiling hesitantly.

"Tonight, we have herb-crusted lamb chops, roast baby potatoes with wild mushrooms, and cherry tomato salad with mozzarella vinaigrette. For dessert, I made cranberry crumb squares."

"You went all out tonight," Ted said.

"I knew we were having company," Summer said, eyeing Chip.

Ted dropped a twenty-dollar bill in the coffee can. Then he held out his plate and encouraged Chip to do the same. Before they walked away, Ted asked Summer, "Join us for a glass of wine later?"

"Absolutely."

They ate at Ted's new outdoor table.

Chip's knife cut through the crispy outer edge of the juicy medium rare chop. He moaned as flavors rolled around his tongue. "Goddamn, Ted, this is outstanding. How often does she do this?"

"Almost every night." Ted said matter-of-factly.

"You eat like this every night? No wonder you want to stay here. She's amazing. What's her story?"

Ted didn't feel right talking about Summer. Instead, he replied, "Just another camper enjoying the peaceful outdoors."

Ted steered the dinner conversation away from Summer and back to business. There were certain bits of information about clients and strategies he wished to discuss in order to provide Chip with a seamless transition, and he didn't want any part of the business transfer to linger.

As Chip took the final bite of the tart, crumbly fruit square, he sighed. "Damn, I wonder if she is for hire?"

Ted laughed. "Not a chance."

"Everybody's got their price," Chip said with conviction.

"Well, then, you should ask her when she comes over."

As the sun retreated for the evening, Ted plugged in his outdoor lights and built a fire. Anticipating Summer's arrival, he moved one of the chairs from the table close to the firepit.

He opened a bottle of Cabernet and poured it into a crystal decanter, another item from his recent online purchase, to allow the wine to breathe.

Chip poured himself scotch, which he had brought with him, and watched with amusement as Ted made his preparations.

"What are you smiling at?" Ted asked.

"You. You know, it was your compulsive attention to detail that made me decide to join your firm."

"You mean I didn't win you over with my charming personality?"

"You never even said hello to me. You just sat down and started peppering me with questions," Chip chuckled.

"I had to get it right. Besides, I was giving you a chance to make up for your socks."

"My socks?"

"Yes," Ted teased. "Who the heck wears red and black checkered socks to an interview?"

"Those were my power socks. See where they got me?"

"Drinking expensive scotch in the middle of wine country?"

"Exactly!" Chip raised his glass.

As she crossed the lane to Ted's site, Summer clutched her half-filled wine glass. Both men stood as she approached.

"Oh, a couple of gentlemen. Thank you."

Ted pointed her to the empty chair between them.

Chip waited until Summer sat before sitting. His gaze lingered before he asked, "Have we met before?"

"I don't believe so," Summer replied.

"You look awfully familiar."

"I have that kind of face," she smiled, then glanced toward Ted and held up her glass. "I couldn't wait. I poured myself a glass while I cleaned up from dinner. Ted, your lights look beautiful."

Ted beamed. "Thank you." He poured himself some wine.

Summer smiled as she watched him pour from his new decanter.

"Summer, I must tell you that was the most amazing dinner I've had in a long time. And I eat, almost nightly, at some of the finest Boston restaurants," Chip said.

"Thank you, Chip. It's one of my greatest joys in life to cook for people."

Chip shot Ted a sideways glance. "I wondered, would you be looking for employment as a personal chef?"

With an abrupt roar, Summer turned to Ted, "Did you put him up to that?"

Ted smirked as he shook his head. "No, he's serious."

"I thank you for the thought, Chip. But it would take a catastrophic occurrence for me to ever feel the need to give up my freedom and go back to the working world."

Ted spread his hands and lifted his brows to extend an *I-told-you-so* look toward Chip.

"That's too bad," Chip said. "Your talents are wasted on a man like Ted—a peanut butter and jelly aficionado."

"I hear congratulations are in order," Summer said, ignoring Chip's comment. She raised her wine glass and tapped his.

"Thank you. I only hope I can live up to Ted's expectations," Chip said warmly.

"The only expectations you need to live up to now are your own. I'm officially out," Ted said.

"What did Marci say when you told her?" Summer asked.

"I haven't told her," Ted replied. "I wanted to wait until it was finished."

"Ted," Summer barked, "you need to call her right now. This decision affects her as much as you."

"I'll call her tomorrow," Ted said.

Summer sighed. "If you wait until tomorrow, how do you think that will make her feel? Honestly, Ted. Sometimes it is very clear that you don't know how to communicate with people."

Ted thought about Summer's observation, then said with a sheepish look, "You're right. I should have told her. Excuse me."

Ted stood, reached for his cell phone, and stepped into the motorhome.

SUMMER

Chip looked at Summer with an open mouth and raised brows.

"Is something wrong?" Summer asked.

"Ah, no. I'm just wondering how you did that."

"Did what?"

"Changed Ted's mind so quickly. He usually needs to analyze an issue from every direction before changing his course of action."

"Even when it is the right thing to do?"

"Yes." Chip replied. "How long have you two known each other?"

"Oh, I don't know. About a month I suppose."

"So, how do you know Marci?"

"She and the family came to visit. What a beautiful family."

Tilting his head, Chip asked, "Are you sure we've never met before?" Chip asked.

"I can't imagine where we might have. Why?"

"I'm not sure. There's something about you that makes me feel like we have."

"Well, they say everyone has a doppelganger. I sure feel sorry for mine," Summer chuckled.

"On the contrary. I see a beautiful, talented, and persuasive woman who knows what she wants out of life."

"Ted warned me you were a smooth talker," Summer smiled.

"What else did he tell you about me?"

"Only that you graduated from Harvard top of your class and that you are a great lawyer."

"Well," Chip said, "I was overconfident, overeager, and over my head. I was lucky enough to make the right choice signing with Ted. I owe him a great deal."

"We are all indebted to each other, Chip. It's the way of the world." Summer raised her glass and took a sip.

Ted returned from the camper with a satisfied smile.

"Well?" Summer asked.

"You were right. She gave me a hard time for not telling her my intentions, but she is very happy. She wanted me to say hello to both of you," Ted said. "She also said we must make an interesting trio and she wished she were here."

Ted and Chip spent the next hour sharing stories from the past. Summer enjoyed hearing about Ted's work. As she listened, the more she understood how difficult the decision for him to retire must have been.

As it came upon nine o'clock, Summer announced she would be turning in.

"So soon?" Chip asked.

"I'm an early riser. Besides, if I don't go to bed now, you won't have cinnamon buns in the morning," she laughed.

"You're in for a treat, Chip. Summer's cinnamon buns are a masterpiece," Ted said, his gaze focused squarely on Summer.

"That coming from a peanut butter and jelly aficionado," Summer chuckled. "Goodnight."

The men stood and said goodnight, then returned to their chairs.

TED

Ted's eyes followed Summer until she was safely inside her camper.

"She's terrific, Ted. Are you two, you know—together?"

Ted quickly replied, "No, nothing like that. We're good friends, that's all. She has led an interesting life. It's nice to have someone my own age to talk to, although I suspect she is younger than I am."

"I can't shake the feeling I've met her before."

"You think you know everybody," Ted chuckled.

"It'll come to me," Chip assured.

In the morning, the heavenly odor of cinnamon buns swirled in the air.

"I couldn't wake up to this every morning. I'd be fifty pounds heavier," Chip told Ted.

"It is a struggle sometimes. But I think Summer is going overboard for your benefit. She's been cooking quite healthy lately," Ted replied.

"Really. Is there any particular reason for that?" Chip asked with a grin.

"Get over it, Chip. There's nothing there."

Over coffee and cinnamon buns, Summer, Ted, and Chip continued their easy conversation from the previous night. Summer showed Chip her VW van and Shasta camper, pointing out the upgrades she had installed.

In the corner of her camper sat a large stack of small brown cardboard boxes. Each box sported the Case Candle logo.

"You really like candles, huh?" Chip asked.

Summer laughed, "Yes, I really do."

From outside the trailer, Ted listened to their conversation and snickered. He decided he would be very disappointed if Chip didn't put two and two together.

Chip was about to exit the tiny trailer when he shouted, "Son-of-a-bitch!" Then he slammed his head on the doorway entrance. Rubbing his forehead, he said, "That's where I've seen you before."

Summer and Ted shared a smile.

Chip stepped out of the camper. "It was graduation day. Arnold Case of Case Candles was the commencement speaker. He gave an incredible speech, and I made it a point to catch up with him after the ceremony. I introduced myself, and he introduced me to,— Chip turned and gaped at Summer "—his wife, Summer. Holy shit!"

Ted roared with laughter while Summer seemed uncomfortable as the object of Chip's revelation.

Chip continued, "Didn't you just sell . . ."

"Yes, I did." Summer cut him off.

"For a whopping . . ."

"Uh huh."

Chip once again put his hand to his forehead then shook his head. "And I offered you a job. I feel like an idiot."

Still chuckling, Ted said, "Well now I can die happy. I would have paid good money to hear those words."

"And you knew," Chip said to Ted.

"Of course," Ted replied.

"And you let me make an ass of myself."

"It was my greatest moment," Ted grinned.

"It was very flattering, Chip. Nobody made an ass out of anybody," Summer interjected.

"Well, Summer, the offer still stands. If you ever need anyone to cook for, I'll be waiting," Chip grinned.

Later, after Chip had loaded his car and was ready to leave, he told Ted, "I'll be right back. I'm just going to go say goodbye to Summer."

Ted waited by Chip's car.

SUMMER

"I can't tell you how nice it was to meet you . . . again," Chip laughed. "I had great respect for your husband and for you. And I'm so happy you and Ted have become friends. But, between you and me . . . I think Ted is crazy about you." Chip winked and kissed her on the cheek.

Summer stood with her mouth agape.

Chip walked back to Ted and shook hands before getting into his car and driving away.

THE PACT

SUMMER

Summer could feel heat on her cheeks and a flutter in her chest. *Son-of-a-biscuit*, she thought. *Why did Chip have to say that?*

Like a schoolgirl, Summer spent the rest of the morning avoiding Ted. She had been telling herself that her blushing and fluttering were part of growing old, maybe a post-menopausal symptom. *Way, way, post-menopausal*, she considered.

By lunchtime, she realized how silly she was being. Chip had been wrong to think Ted had any interest in her. After all, she and Ted had already discussed the issue over a glass of bourbon. Summer chuckled at the memory, then ventured outside.

Ted sat at his table and concentrated on his laptop. She enjoyed watching him. She imagined him sitting at a desk surrounded by piles of contracts. He had perfect posture and a stately look to him even when wearing jeans instead of a suit. She thought him a handsome man, his graying hair added to his appeal. Once again, Summer thought it unfair that most men seem to age better than women. Her gray hair only made her look old, she thought. And she battled wrinkly, dry skin, while his skin seemed healthy and resilient.

She began to feel flush.

When Ted looked up and saw her standing outside her trailer, he waved her over.

"Are you busy?" he yelled.

"Nope. I'll be over in a few minutes."

Summer returned to her camper and splashed cool water on her face. *A minor hot flash,* she told herself, then brewed a cup of ginger tea and traveled across the way.

"Please don't tell me you're placing another online order. I'd hate to think I had anything to do with turning you into a hoarder," Summer joked.

"On the contrary. I think you should take the day off from cooking tomorrow and we should explore Seneca Lake. I've just been researching the area. It would take weeks to get through all the wineries. And then, I'd like to treat you to dinner after all the meals you've made for me. Dinner out, not my cooking, obviously. The only thing is, we would have to use your vehicle. But I could drive if you wanted me to."

"That sounds great. It's a date!" Summer responded, then quickly added, "I mean, not a date date. What I meant was, it sounds nice. I'd like that."

Ted snickered. "I get it. It's all right. I'm trying not to be so literal about everything. I don't have to be anymore. I'm retired."

"I'll put a note on the bulletin board that I won't be cooking tomorrow night. Then I need to get tonight's dinner started."

"Is there anything I can do to help?" Ted asked.

"Really? Are you serious or just being polite?" Summer asked.

"I'm serious. It might be fun to learn how to cook. Unless you would rather not," Ted added. "I would completely understand if you didn't want me in the way."

"No, this could be fun. Let's get to it," Summer said.

Ted put his laptop away and followed Summer.

"What are we making, anyway?" Ted asked.

"Stuffed bell peppers. But not like you've ever had, I'm sure. These will be a healthy version of the old classic," Summer replied.

"Why doesn't that surprise me?" Ted smiled.

Summer unpacked two white bib aprons from the bottom drawer of her van cabinet and handed one to Ted. Each apron had two wide waist-high pockets and a thin pocket on the left chest for a pencil or small thermometer. Summer showed Ted how to place the neck strap over his head and wrap the waist tie around his body before tying it in front.

"There. Now you look the part. Do you know how to use a knife?" Summer asked.

Ted rolled his eyes and replied, "Of course I do."

Skeptical, Summer retrieved her polypropylene cutting board and placed it in front of Ted. She then handed him an eight-inch Wusthof chef knife.

"It's very sharp, be careful," Summer warned.

Again Ted rolled his eyes.

From the camper, Summer brought a large bag of vegetables and placed them on the table. She laid a sheet pan to Ted's right, then placed an empty paper bag on the ground at Ted's feet.

Summer handed Ted a disposable towelette and a dry towel.

Ted stared at Summer and waited for directions.

"Well, go ahead. Wash and dry your hands," she told him.

Summer did the same, then retrieved red and green peppers from the bag and set them on the table.

Taking the knife from Ted, Summer placed a green pepper on the cutting board and sliced it in half, lengthwise. With her hands, she removed the core and cleaned the pepper of its seeds and excess membrane. She placed the pepper halves on the sheet pan and threw the seeds in the paper bag at Ted's feet. Then she used the knife to remove the small amount of green pepper surrounding the pepper's core and diced it into small pieces. She pushed the small pile of diced peppers to the side then threw the core into the paper bag on the ground.

"Do you see what I did? We don't want to waste any of the pepper. We'll use the diced pieces in the stuffing mix. Do you think you can handle this?" Summer asked.

Visibly annoyed, Ted reached his hand out for the knife. Summer gave it to him, handle first.

Ted placed a green pepper on the cutting board and used his left hand to steady the pepper. He placed the knife on the vegetable and pushed straight down. The pepper collapsed, and the knife rolled just enough for the tip of the blade to slice into the tip of Ted's left index finger.

"Owww! Gosh darn it!" Ted yelled, then stuck his bleeding finger in his mouth.

Summer squinted, then said, "Here, let me see it."

Ted pulled his finger from his mouth to show Summer the slice.

"It's not too bad. You won't need stitches," she said as she pulled a bandage from her apron pocket.

"You just happen to have a bandage in your pocket?" Ted asked.

"I had a feeling." Summer glanced at him as she covered his wound. "So, shall we try this again?"

Summer discarded the crushed pepper and brought the knife and cutting board into the trailer to clean off droplets of Ted's blood. She handed Ted another towelette.

"Watch me again." Summer explained to Ted that, instead of muscling the knife through the food, he should let the knife do the work. She placed the tip of the knife on the core end of the pepper and, keeping her steadying fingertip tucked under her first knuckle, she moved the knife in a gliding motion away from her body. The sharp blade made a crisp, smooth cut.

"Simple," she said, "and no body parts impaled."

After washing his hands, Ted tried again, this time following Summer's instructions.

"Okay," Ted smiled. "I get it," he said as the pepper split nicely on either side of the blade.

It took him twice as long as it would have taken Summer, but she didn't care. If she could have made their time together last all night, she would have. She enjoyed watching Ted with his meticulous nature cutting the peppers as close to evenly as possible and how he kept the surface of the board so clean. She silently giggled when she noticed he bit his lower lip while concentrating. She wondered if he had done the same while working in his office.

Ted sliced and cleaned twelve green and twelve red peppers and stacked them on the sheet pan.

In the meantime, Summer shredded carrots, diced onions, minced garlic, chopped tomatoes, and crumbled cauliflower into small bits.

"Okay. What now?" Ted asked.

"Now you are going to roast the peppers on the grill," Summer replied.

She showed him how to lightly char the skin of the peppers without over-cooking them.

"Why do you do this? Couldn't you just stuff them and bake them?" he asked. "That's what my mother used to do."

"Sure, you could. But this gives them more flavor. You used to watch your mother cook?"

"Yes, sometimes. Mostly she would boil everything. She would even boil summer squash. I remember hating summer squash as a kid, but my father made us eat everything on our plate, so my brother and I suffered through it. The first time Carol cooked for me, she told me she was making summer squash. Of course, I knew I would have to eat it, but I wasn't looking forward to it. I didn't want to be rude. But she cooked it on a charcoal grill with butter and seasonings, which was delicious. It wasn't the mushy stuff I got as a kid."

"I know what you mean. My mother was the same way. I think most women from our parents' generation were taught to cook their food to death. That's probably why my father would only eat hot dogs, well-done hamburgers, and ham." Summer laughed. "I always thought that was one of the reasons I chose to become a chef. I guess I felt that food was getting a bum rap."

With the scalded peppers set aside, Summer replaced the grill top with the stovetop. She retrieved her large cast iron skillet and covered the bottom with olive oil.

They browned the onions, garlic, and carrots until soft before adding the cauliflower and tomatoes to sear but not overcook. Ted stirred the vegetables evenly as Summer instructed.

Then Summer opened a bottle of red wine and poured them each a glass. She found an easy listening station on the radio for background music while she showed Ted how to brown ground turkey without drying it out.

They laughed, they sang, and Summer danced as they combined all the ingredients and seasoned and stuffed the peppers. They added cheese, tomato sauce, and a sparse amount of red wine just for fun.

Ted had his hands elbow deep in the wash sink when Frank Sinatra's classic song, "Moon River," wafted through the speakers.

"Oh, Ted. You have to dance with me," Summer said.

"What? No. I'm not much of a dancer."

"It's my mother's favorite song, and I need you to dance with me," she said, her arms held out in front of her.

Ted paused, then wiped his hands on the dish towel and stepped outside the camper. Sunset was still hours away, but a cloud moved overhead and created the feeling of dusk.

Ted placed his right hand on Summer's waist and, his left hand holding her right, they began to waltz. He slowly steered them away from the table to an open area where they could move more freely. They moved as one as they circled the gravel dance floor, Ted using his right hand to guide Summer, Summer responding with ease.

Unable to speak, Summer once again felt the heat on her face. Not since Arnold had she been so swept away.

The song slowly came to an end as did the dance, and Ted stood holding Summer in his arms, gazing into her eyes and she back at him.

The cloud dissipated and sun shone like a searchlight seeking a suspect. Ted abruptly dropped his arms and took a step back.

Summer could feel fear pulse through him and did her best to diffuse it.

She turned off the music and began to babble. "You are a wonderful dancer, Ted. You and your wife must have made a handsome couple on the dance floor," she said as she moved into her camper to continue washing the dishes. "Arnold had two left feet. We even took lessons once, but he just couldn't get the hang of it. It was about the only thing he wasn't good at. Where did you learn to dance like that?"

Ted didn't answer.

"Ted?"

Silence.

Summer picked up the dish towel and turned while wiping her hands dry to look out the camper door. She caught sight of him just before he closed his motorhome door.

"Stupid, Summer. That was so stupid of you," she whispered. *But it was incredibly wonderful*, she thought.

Trying not to think of Ted freaking out in his camper, she finished cleaning dishes, then prepared dessert.

Fifteen minutes before gong time, she heard a knock on her door.

She swung the door open. "Ted. I didn't expect you to . . ."

"I know," Ted frowned. "Summer, once again and probably not for the last time, I owe you an apology. I have a habit of acting juvenile and running away from . . . things."

Summer stepped outside to join him.

Ted continued. "Not only is it rude, but it's unfair to you, who may or may not be having scary and confusing feelings of your own."

"Scary and confusing? It's that bad, huh?" Summer asked.

"I'm just not fit to be around people. I'm kind of a mess," Ted said. "I really enjoy your company, but I panic when things get a little . . . familiar."

Summer's heart tugged.

"Well, Ted, you may be a mess, but you have gotten awful good at apologizing." Summer smiled. "What if we do this? What if we make a pact that, no matter what, you and I will never be more than friends? That way we can dance, laugh, sing, and even walk arm-in-arm without any consequences. No guilt, no scary and confusing feelings, just full out friendship. How does that sound?"

"A pact? Do you mean like a contract?" Ted was skeptical.

"Sure, a contract. I'll even cut my finger and rub it against your bleeding finger to make it official," Summer grinned.

"I don't think that will be necessary," Ted laughed. "A pact. Hmmm. Okay, I'm in."

"Shall we shake hands or hug on it?" Summer asked.

"Let's start with a handshake," Ted said. "Who knows what kind of reaction my dysfunctional brain will have if we hug."

Summer shook Ted's hand, all the while thinking she'd rather have some of Ted than no Ted at all. And she felt sure that's where things had been heading. Her schoolgirl crush or whatever it was she was feeling, would have to stay just that, a crush.

Summer handed Ted the gong mallet and said, "Time for dinner."

Ted gripped the mallet. Then, with the tip of his tongue sticking out of the corner of his mouth, he walloped the gong.

He stood beside Summer and helped her serve twenty-one hungry campers—each getting one stuffed green and one red pepper on top of a mound of spaghetti and sauce. They served dessert on a separate paper plate.

First in line were Jerry and Judy from next door.

"Where's Seamus?" Ted asked.

"Far away from the food," Judy laughed.

Next, Summer introduced Ted to Harry, the salesman from Ohio.

"The artichoke man?" Ted asked.

"She told you about that, huh?" Harry asked.

"She did," Ted smiled.

"Harry sells winery equipment," Summer said.

"Oh, yeah? You mean machinery?" Ted asked.

"Yes, and tools. Our biggest sellers are the hydraulic presses, but we sell destemmers and crushers as well," Harry replied.

"Someday I'd like to see how that operation works," Ted said.

"I'm sure you could get one of the local wineries to give you a peek at the inside operation. It was nice to meet you," Harry said, making way for the next person in line as he headed back to his campsite with a full plate and dessert.

Summer knew each one of them by name and introduced Ted to those he hadn't already met. They shared a short, pleasant conversation with most of the diners.

After everyone including them were fed and the serving dishes and pots and pans cleaned, Ted and Summer sat at Summer's table. Ted asked, "When did you find time to make the angel food cake?"

Summer let go a chuckle, then replied, "I'll tell you a little secret. You already know I love to cook. I cook when I'm happy, and I cook when I'm sad. But I find I do my best and most ambitious cooking when I'm worried about something or someone." She cast him a glance, then continued. "I once made a five-tiered red velvet cake depicting ascension into heaven. It was the most beautiful and ornate cake I've ever made, and nobody ever saw it. It only took me four hours."

"Wow! That must have been an incredible cake."

"It should have taken me a lot longer. So, to answer your question, when you abruptly left this afternoon, I baked a cake," Summer grinned.

Ted pursed his lips in shame, then asked, "What were you worried about that day you made the ascension cake?"

"The presidential election," Summer replied with a snicker.

Ted grinned, "Which one?"

"Ted, I think we should amend our pact to include that you and I will never talk politics."

"Good point. I vote yea on the amendment," Ted grinned.

"The yeas have it," Summer smiled. "How about a glass of wine?"

"What took you so long?"

MINCING WORDS

SUMMER

The following day, Ted drove them in the VW bus to Seneca Lake, stopping at wineries and points of interest. By special request, Ted got his chance to see backroom workings of one of the local wineries, and the process fascinated him. It felt like spring break from the world of adulthood, albeit in responsible fashion. The designated driver, Ted bought a bottle of every wine that Summer recommended from the tastings so he could try them later.

Without any thoughts or worries about time, they leisurely strolled through vineyards and parks. They had a late morning snack at a café and an early dinner at a lakeside resort. They sipped coffee and watched the sunset from a boat ramp in Watkins Glen.

Topics of conversation included childhoods, marriages, successes, and failures. Summer had no trepidation about sharing her life events and did most of the talking earlier in the day. But as the afternoon progressed, Summer's openness ebbed in order to encourage Ted to reveal personal anecdotes.

He spoke of the day Marci was born and how they almost didn't make it to the hospital in time and how Carol used to sing in the shower. He told how he sat on the edge of their bed and listened, never knowing if Carol knew.

Summer responded with admission of her inability to carry a tune and her indifference to others knowing it. They shared a laugh.

Summer spoke of her miscarriages and ensuing attempts at using medical science to have her own child. They shared the somber moment.

Not once did they talk about business or work. And true to their pact, they only skirted the edge of politics, each respecting the other's view on social and financial issues as they found they weren't so different after all.

When Ted turned off the engine of the Volkswagen in front of Summer's camper, neither one moved. It was dark. Not thinking they would be back so late they had left that morning without leaving any lights on.

"I had a wonderful time today, Ted. That was probably the best day I've had since I lost Arnold. Thank you," Summer said as she choked up.

"For me, too. I didn't think I'd ever be able to enjoy myself again. Or maybe I thought I shouldn't. I don't know. But today, for the first time since Carol, I felt I could relax." Ted cleared his throat. "Imagine that?"

"Imagine that," Summer repeated.

From the backseat, Ted retrieved the six bottles of wine he had purchased.

"Goodnight, Summer."

"Goodnight, Ted."

✦

Each day during the following week, Ted continued to help Summer cook dinner, though he was more of a hinderance than help as she taught him the trade. But Summer didn't mind. She loved sharing her passion with Ted. And he got better at handling a knife.

A week after their Seneca Lake jaunt, Summer had just finished her morning meditation when a shiny black Lincoln SUV stopped in front of Ted's camper. As soon as it pulled up, she saw Ted rush out the door. He smiled like a boy on the last day of school. A woman stepped out of the vehicle, and Summer tensed. Ted spoke with her for a moment before circling the car. Then he returned to the woman's side.

Summer heard the two laugh and cringed. Standing so she could see better, Summer focused on the well-dressed woman who wore a business suit and looked as if she had just stepped out of a boardroom. She very much presented herself as a female version of Ted, and he seemed quite comfortable conversing with her.

A tightness formed in Summer's chest as she scrutinized their interaction. Her jaw began to ache as she realized that she had been clenching her teeth.

What the hell is the matter with me? Summer thought. She recognized the emotion. She hadn't felt jealous since Robbie Sanders asked her friend Betsy to the fifth grade Spring dance instead of asking her. Then she recalled poor Betsy sitting against the wall, alone on a bench the entire night while Robbie hung out with his friends, never once asking Betsy to dance.

Summer chastised herself. *Jealousy is a useless emotion, Summer, and Ted is your friend.*

A moment later, a blue Lincoln sedan pulled behind the SUV, and the woman walked over, got into the passenger seat, and the car drove away.

Ted glanced in Summer's direction, smiled, and said, "What do you think?"

"What do I think about what?"

"My new car?"

"Your new . . . ?" Relieved, Summer released a heavy sigh. Then, realizing Ted hadn't left the campground since the two went to Seneca Lake, she asked, "Did you buy this car online? Without seeing it?"

"Yes. It's a Lincoln, brand new and American made. I did the research, checked reviews, compared models, and came up with this. It's a beauty, isn't it?"

"What . . . why?" asked Summer.

"Well, I can't keep bothering you every time I need to go somewhere. And now I can get back to see some of Frankie's baseball games. I can leave the motorhome here and drive back home whenever I need to."

"Look at you, Ted, making plans," Summer said with a grin.

"Well, the possibility for plans, anyway," Ted laughed.

"It's very nice, but how does it drive?"

"I have no idea. What do you say we take it for a ride?"

"All right. Let's go," Summer said as she opened the passenger door and got in.

Ted started the engine, then fixed the seat and mirror positions. Summer watched him as he took note of the location of all switches, knobs, and levers. Then they were on their way.

"It's very comfortable," Summer said. "It's like I'm sitting on a cloud. I'm beginning to realize how far vehicles have come since they made the VW bus. Is this real leather?"

"Yes, it is," Ted chuckled. "Your seat is heated, too. See that button there?" Ted pointed to the dashboard. "Press it."

Summer felt the warmth on her back and bottom. "Oh, I could take a nap right here."

"I should have done this weeks ago," Ted said.

"It's good timing, Ted. I've got to go away for a few days. Maybe more," Summer said. "I have this obligation in Boston that I can't get out of."

"Oh? Something good I hope."

"Yes." Summer paused. "It's for something good. But I must say I'm not happy about having to go. I just wish they would let me send someone else in my place, but they insisted."

"They who?"

"Harvard Medical School and others."

"Harvard? What's happening at Harvard?"

"A project to do with my philanthropic foundation. I tried to get out of it, but I need to sign some papers and such."

"What kind of project?"

"A fertility clinic for families with limited means. It was the first thing I did when I decided to sell the business. And now they're ready to open. The grand opening is next week."

"Wow. Why haven't you mentioned this before?" Ted asked.

"I'm not sure. Maybe because it brings up a lot of confusing emotions. I guess ignoring them is my way of running away from them."

Ted steered the SUV into a scenic lookout area and turned off the engine.

"I have an idea," he said. "Let me drive you to Boston. You can stay in the guest room at my house and use my other car to go wherever you need. And I can visit with Marci and the boys. What do you think?"

"No, Ted. I couldn't let you do that. It's too much trouble."

"It's no trouble. I planned on going back to visit anyway. This way, neither one of us has to make the trip alone."

"Well, that part makes sense. But I can't stay at your house."

"Why not?"

"Because it wouldn't be right. What would Marci think? And the boys? And your neighbors?"

"First of all, I don't give a hoot-and-a-holler about the neighbors, and Marci and the boys like you. They would be thrilled to see you again. Unless you're looking for an excuse because you don't want to stay. Then, I completely understand."

"No, it's not that. I'm just worried that you're making this offer now and once you think about it, you'll regret it and be too polite to say so."

Ted smiled. "I admit, that does sound like me. But that was the old me. That was pre-contract Ted."

"Are you positive?"

"Yes."

"And you'll tell me if you change your mind?"

"Yes."

"Okay," Summer said. "Let's give the neighbors something to hoot-and-holler about."

The day before the grand opening, Summer and Ted packed up the new SUV and headed for Ted's home in Newton, just outside of Boston. Ted had called ahead and asked that Marci go to his house and get the main guest room ready for Summer. To say Marci was surprised would be an understatement.

They pulled out of the campground at 9:30 a.m.

"So, tell me about the clinic," Ted said as he drove.

"It sounded like a good idea at the time, but I'm beginning to wish I never started this whole thing."

"What do you mean?"

"Don't get me wrong. The clinic will be wonderful. But I thought I could just donate the money in Arnold's memory and not have to make any public appearances."

"You've managed to stay out of the spotlight your whole life. Why did you agree to this?"

"The woman who is organizing the grand opening has been hounding me to attend. She wouldn't take no for an answer. She also mentioned that some of the primary investors insist that I be there. She called again two weeks ago and said I had some legal papers to sign at the dedication. If I want the clinic to open, I have no choice but to show up and sign the damned papers."

"Well, maybe it won't be so bad. You can make a quick appearance, take a few photos, sign papers, and be gone," Ted said.

Summer was not convinced.

"When is the last time you were in Boston?" Ted asked, trying to change the subject.

"Last year, when I sold the business," Summer replied.

Conversation then involved scheduling bathroom breaks, making lunch choices, figuring out directions, and small talk.

With two quick stops, the trip took five and a half hours. They were in the house with the car unpacked by 3:15 that afternoon.

"Ted, this is beautiful," Summer said of the house.

"Thank you. Carol did all the decorating, of course."

"I can tell. I would never imagine that you would purchase a Michael Mazur original painting," Summer said as she pointed to the framed artwork hanging above the living room fireplace.

"And you would be wrong. I purchased that painting at a fundraiser in Provincetown and gave it to Carol as an anniversary present."

"I'm impressed."

"Finally," Ted said, lightheartedly. "Here." He lifted Summer's suitcase. "Let me show you to your room."

Summer followed Ted up the wide, curved stairway off the foyer. On the right at the top of the stairs, the door stood open. The smell of fresh roses drifted out.

A bouquet of fresh flowers, roses among them, met Summer. "How in the world did you manage that?"

"Marci. I asked her to get the room ready. She tends to go over the top sometimes."

"They are beautiful, and so is the room," Summer said.

"Good. I'm glad you like it. You have your own bathroom." Ted pointed to an open doorway on the other side of the room. "My room is down the end of the hall if you need me. Can I get you anything?"

"No, I'm fine. I'm going to unpack and then bounce on the bed. I'll meet you downstairs?"

Ted chuckled and nodded. "Please, make yourself at home. I want you to feel comfortable here."

Summer smiled. "Thank you, Ted."

TED

Ted texted Marci to let her know they had arrived. Twenty minutes later, Marci and the boys were in his kitchen.

"Hey, Grandpa, who's cool car is that in the driveway?" Frankie asked.

"That's my new SUV. Do you like it?" Ted asked.

"Heck, yeah. It's a Lincoln. Can I sit in it?" Frankie asked.

"Me, too, Grandpa. I want to sit in it, too," Casey said, jumping up and down.

"Sure, go check it out," Ted said.

Marci warned, "Be careful. If you scratch it or tear anything, I will not be happy."

"Geez, Mom. We're just gonna sit in it," Frankie said as they went outside.

"So?" Marci asked.

"So, what?"

"So, what's going on with you and Summer?" Marci asked.

"Summer and I are good friends, Marci. That's all we'll ever be, so stop trying to make anything of it. But there are a few things I should tell you about her."

Ted hadn't yet told Marci about Summer's ownership and then sale of Case Candles. He knew Marci would recognize the brand, as she had many of their candles in her own home, as did most people in New England.

Marci's eyes grew wider and wider as he explained Summer's circumstances, financial status, and foundation.

"So, tomorrow is the grand opening of the new fertility clinic her foundation built. That's why we are here. And to visit you, of course," Ted finished.

Marci's mouth lay open like a baby's waiting for its next spoonful of food.

At that moment, Summer walked into the kitchen.

"Hello, Marci," Summer said. "What's wrong? Did I interrupt something?"

"I just told her about Case Candles, the sale of the business, and your foundation."

Summer cackled, "Oh. I guess it is a bit of a shocker" She turned to Marci. "Let me make you a cup of tea. Do you have tea, Ted?"

"In the drawer under the coffee pot."

Summer went directly to the cabinet that held the coffee and teacups. She also found the kettle without any trouble.

"Carol set up a proper kitchen. Everything is where it should be," she said.

Ted received a questioning glance from Marci.

He placed his hand on top of Marci's and said, "I've told her all about your mother. And she's told me all about her husband."

Summer turned. "I'm sorry, Marci. Have I made this uncomfortable for you?"

Marci smiled and said, "No, you two have just thrown a lot of information at me, and I need time to process it."

"Ah, she is her father's daughter."

The comment caused the three to fall into laughter.

"Hey, what's so funny? Hi, Summer," Casey said when he bounded through the kitchen door with Frankie Jr. close behind.

"Hello, Casey. Hello Frankie," Summer said.

"Hello," Frankie said quietly, his eyes fixated on the kitchen floor.

Ted and Summer exchanged amused glances.

"How do you like my car?" Ted asked.

"It's neat. I like the way it smells," Casey said.

"What about you, Frankie?" Ted asked.

"Yeah," Frankie answered, still not looking up.

Marci squinted. "Do you feel all right, Frankie?"

Frankie nodded.

"He's fine. He just has car envy, that's all. Why don't you boys go downstairs and play some pool," Ted said.

"Can we, Mom?" Casey asked.

"Yes. Just don't touch anything you're not supposed to."

Summer served herself and Marci tea.

"I assumed you did not want any tea, Ted."

"You assumed correctly."

"Do you think Frankie will ever be able to look me in the eye?" Summer asked Ted.

"Ohhh, that's what that was all about," Marci said.

"Maybe someday," Ted said. "But imagery like that stays with a boy forever."

"Even if he didn't see anything?" Marci asked.

"That's even better. He created the perfect picture in his head. And he will recall that picture many times in the future." Ted clasped his hands behind his head and smiled.

"For chrissake, Dad, really? Did you have to?" Marci winced.

"Don't swear, Marci," Ted said.

Summer's cheeks turned the color of passion, the same color of a young boy blushing while discovering his manhood.

Ted and Summer spent the remainder of the day in quietude, occasionally engaging in comfortable yet casual conversation before retiring early.

⟋⟍ ⟋⟍

The next morning, Ted had coffee ready by the time Summer came downstairs.

"Good morning," he said from his seat at the kitchen table. "Can I get you some coffee?"

"Good morning. No. You sit still. I can get it myself."

Ted had his laptop open to catch up on the news.

"You've been holding out on me," Ted said.

Summer asked, "What do you mean?"

"You've talked about this fertility clinic like it's not a big deal. Like it's some office building. This is a massive, state-of-the-art medical and research facility with the finest doctors and scientific researchers in the country. It's bigger than most hospitals."

"Well, I didn't say it wasn't," Summer replied.

"Have you seen the list of people who are attending this grand opening today? It's a who's who of medical, political, business, and philanthropic worlds combined."

"I know. That's why I didn't want to go," Summer said, backing herself into the kitchen counter.

"Hey," Ted asked, "are you all right?"

"No. I don't want to do this. Why do they need me there? My lawyers can handle all the paperwork. It's going to be a dog and pony show, and I don't know if I'm supposed to be the dog or the pony. This is exactly the kind of publicity I've been avoiding my whole life."

Ted rose and joined Summer at the counter. "I didn't realize. I'm sorry. I thought you were just being humble. You really hate this kind of thing, don't you? That's why you never went with Arnold to the fundraisers and grand openings."

"I have more in common with the people who will be using the clinic than the people attending the ceremony. I don't fit into their political agendas and high society gatherings, and I don't wish to. Arnold took care of all that."

"And you stayed in the background."

"That's right. But Arnold can't help me with this one," Summer sadly stated.

"No, but I can if you want me to."

Summer closed her eyes, smiled, and nodded. Then she said, "They want me to speak, Ted."

"Oh, I see. Okay. Well." Ted could feel Summer's anxiety. "Have you got a speech?"

Summer shook her head.

"Do you have anyone on your team to write one for you?" he asked.

"What team? I have lawyers. And you know what they're like, no offense," Summer said.

Ted chuckled, "None taken."

"I'm sorry. I thought if I just got here, I'd find a way. But I'm terrified. Not of those people. I don't give a rat's ass about them, but I'm afraid of letting Arnold down. I don't know that I can get through a speech without . . . breaking down. Or I may go the other way and insult everyone in the audience."

"Those aren't your only options," Ted grinned. "Let's sit down and talk about it. Tell me why you wanted to build this facility."

After two cups of coffee with Ted asking questions, he figured he had extracted enough information along with what he read online to create a short speech for Summer.

"We'll take this one step at a time," Ted said. Then he heard a car pull into the driveway. "Who could be here this early?"

"It's Marci," Summer said. "She's taking me shopping. I don't have a decent outfit for this thing."

"Perfect. I'll take care of everything else. Don't worry. We'll make it as painless as possible. You'll be in and out of there before you realize it. I just need the name and number of the contact person," Ted said.

"Here," Summer said as she texted Ted the woman's information.

Marci came through the door wearing a happy smile. "Are you ready for a shopping spree?"

"Let me get my coat and purse. I'll be right back," Summer said.

Once Summer left the room, Ted said, "Marci, she's very nervous about today. Make sure she dresses comfortably. That always makes these things easier. How busy do you think Frank is this morning?"

"He can usually make some free time. Why?"

"I may need help writing a speech."

"She has to speak? No wonder she's so nervous. Don't worry. I'll try to make this fun," Marci said.

"The grand opening is set for 4:30. Summer needs to be there by 4:00," Ted said.

"We've got plenty of time," Marci replied.

Summer and Marci left the house, and Ted jumped into action. He dialed Mrs. Grace Weatherby's phone number, the contact Summer had given him.

"Hello, Mrs. Weatherby. My name is Theodore Winter. I will be assisting Summer with her itinerary today. If you don't mind, I have a few questions."

After their conversation, Ted called Dan.

"Dan, good morning. It's Ted."

"Good morning, Ted. Is everything all right?"

"Yes, everything is fine. Could you come by the house this morning? I could use your help with something."

"I've got a ten o'clock tee time. I could shoot over now if that works," Dan asked.

"I would really appreciate it. You're the best. See you soon."

Ted hung up and called Frank. Frank told Ted he would be right over.

With the three sitting at Ted's kitchen table, Ted explained the situation.

"We need a short speech to cover the personal, medical, and communal reasons why this facility is so important, and it should include some of these points." Ted pointed to the pad of paper he used to record Summer's thoughts from that morning. "Frank, you have the marketing angle. Dan, you have the medical knowledge, and I've got the personal story. Among the three of us, we should be able to handle this. We also need to keep in mind that Summer is terrified about this, so let's keep it as short, simple, and honest as possible."

GRACE VS. GRACE

SUMMER

Marci drove Summer to Newbury Street in Boston where fine boutiques and salons thrive. While visiting three clothing stores in just over two hours, Marci distracted Summer with stories about her and her family. She told how she and Frank met at a laundromat and went to a nearby café while their clothes dried. She talked of the boys' strengths and weaknesses and how unprepared she felt being the mother of a teenager. She kept the mood light and fun. While enjoying their conversations, Summer chose her dress, shoes, and accessories.

"All right. What do you think about your hair?" Marci asked.

"I hadn't thought about it," Summer said shakily.

"Let's see if we can get lucky with one of these salons. They usually require an appointment."

The first salon was booked, but when they inquired about an appointment at the second, the receptionist told them Paolo had just had a noon cancellation. Could they come back then? the woman asked.

"What do you think?" Marci asked Summer.

"I feel like a prized pig getting ready for the fair. But I suppose I need to do something with my hair. Okay, let's do it," Summer sighed.

The young receptionist giggled, "We'll get you in blue ribbon form, honey."

"Well, then. Paolo will need to be a miracle worker," Summer replied.

"There's none better," she said. "We'll see you at noon."

Summer insisted on treating Marci to an early lunch. Newbury Street also hosted some of Boston's best restaurants and cafés. They chose a café with glass front windows so they could watch the outdoor activity.

"I don't know how to thank you for your help, Marci. This whole thing is very unnerving for me. If it weren't so important, I would turn around and go back to my little trailer right now," Summer admitted.

"I admire what you are doing, Summer. Going outside of your comfort zone takes courage."

"Courage? No. It takes insanity," Summer laughed.

"Think about all the people who will benefit from the clinic. Focus on them. Maybe that will help get you through it," Marci said.

Summer noticed Marci's attention drifting.

"Would you excuse me?" Marci said. "I'm going to go to the ladies' room."

Summer feared she had interrupted Marci's daily routine. She hoped she hadn't caused a problem. She felt guilty that her obligation had inconvenienced both Marci and Ted.

Marci was back in her chair in time to order a cobb salad and tea. Summer opted for roasted chicken and vegetable soup to soothe her nerves.

"Is everything all right? Am I keeping you from something important? I feel terrible for taking up your time," Summer said.

"Absolutely not! I'm happy to be here with you. I haven't had a proper girls' day out in ages. So, what would you like to do with your hair? Do you want to color it?" Marci asked.

"No. I don't like the idea of a lot of chemicals in my hair. But I do need a cut and style, something simple and easy to take care of. That's how I live my life these days."

"Hardly," Marci retorted. "You cook for everyone, and you go on adventures. Dad told me about your beekeeping day. Now that would have unnerved me," Marci winced.

"All things I love. It took me sixty-five years to make the time to do the things Arnold and I should have been doing all along—living life in joy and happiness instead of chasing success and, ultimately, money. Although Arnold loved his work, I wish we had taken more time for ourselves. I suppose the key is a question of balance."

"I know what you mean, but it's so hard to find that balance."

"I suppose it's meant to be hard," Summer tilted her head and peered outside as if the answer lay there. "Maybe that's one of the lessons I am on this earth to learn, and I believe I have."

"What if you were put on this earth to do what you are doing today?" Marci asked as she placed her hand on top of Summer's.

Summer straightened her back and again looked out the window. When she returned her gaze to Marci, she had tears in her eyes. "I hadn't thought of it that way." Summer topped Marci's hand with her other and sighed, "Thank you."

Paolo was ready for them when they arrived back at the salon.

"Sugar, you just come right on over here so I can get a look at you," Paolo crooned, his voice as soft as a feather duster as he directed her to his chair.

Summer glanced at Marci, and an easy smile replaced her anxious state.

"Uh huh, hmmm, okay," Paolo said as he lifted, spread, and tested the texture of Summer's hair. "What did you have in mind, sweetie?"

"Paolo, here is the deal. I have to speak in front of a large crowd of overpaid lawyers, underpaid hospital staff, and ultra-ego politicians.

And I am scared to death. So, you need to make me look fantastic but not pretentious, elegant but not snobbish, and mature but not weathered. Can you do that?"

"Sweet pea, you let me make you a blonde, and I'll turn you into Christie Brinkley on a swimsuit runway."

Summer chuckled, "This old body hasn't seen a swimsuit in twenty-five years. Let's say we keep the gray and do the best you can with what I've got. Not too short and no bangs. Everything else is fair game."

"All right, honey. But if I may make one tiny suggestion?" Paolo asked.

"Yes?"

"I can brighten your gray hair with a few highlights. If we do that, I promise you will look exquisite."

Summer glanced at Marci, who shrugged her shoulders.

"Okay, Paolo. Highlights it is," Summer sighed as she sat back in the chair.

An hour and fifteen minutes later, Summer stepped onto the Newbury Street sidewalk feeling reborn. Paolo had been true to his word, and Summer rewarded him handsomely for it.

"One more stop for fingernail polish and then back to Dad's," Marci said.

"It's hardly worth it, Marci. My nails are a mess." Summer flexed her arthritic fingers to examine them.

"Nothing a little shaping and polishing won't cure."

The house was empty when Summer and Marci got back. Marci filed and shaped Summer's nails, painting them blue to match her outfit. Then the two went upstairs to get Summer dressed.

"It's getting late," Summer said, eyeing the clock reading 2:55. "I wonder where your father is."

"He'll be here. We don't need to leave for another half hour or so," Marci said confidently. "Besides, I could always drive you if he is stuck somewhere."

On the verge of expressing her fear of going to the grand opening without Ted, Summer heard the kitchen door open and close.

"Dad, is that you?" Marci called.

"Who else would it be?" he called back.

"Thank God," Summer sighed.

"I'm going to go talk to Dad. You look beautiful," Marci smiled.

Summer took her by both hands and said, "Thank you for everything, Marci."

TED

Ted stood by the sink drinking a glass of water when Marci bounded down the stairs and into the kitchen. He wore his finest business suit.

"Where have you been?" Marci whispered. "We were worried you wouldn't make it here in time. I called you from the café. Did you get the message?"

"I had an errand to run," Ted said, "Yes, I got your message and made the arrangements. It was a great idea. I wish I had thought of it myself. How did the shopping go?"

Marci smiled. Summer had made her way downstairs and stood in the kitchen behind Ted.

"You tell me," Marci said as she bobbed her head toward Summer.

Ted turned and took in Summer. His eyes widened, and his lips parted. He stood frozen.

She looked stunning in a peacock blue wrap-around dress with soft pleats at the waist and a string of pearls accentuating the V-neck design.

She wore matching low-heeled pumps, and around her shoulders lay a multicolored pashmina with hues of blue, magenta, jade, and orange. Tousles of curls framed her face while a loose braid gathered her hair in back. It seemed to shimmer in the daylight.

Still motionless, he locked his eyes on hers. Ted cleared his throat and said, "You look beautiful." Remembering Marci stood behind him, Ted clumsily set down his glass of water, averted his eyes, and shuffled his feet.

"Thank you, Ted. You look mighty handsome yourself," Summer smiled.

Ted brushed his hand down the front of his suitcoat. "Italian made," he said awkwardly.

"So is mine," Summer replied.

At that moment, Ted identified with Frankie's predicament when it came to Summer. And it scared the hell out of him.

"I've got to get home," Marci said as she hugged Summer. "Good luck."

"Thank you, again, Marci. I don't know what I would have done without you," Summer said.

Ted took the moment to gather himself. Once Marci had left, he went over the itinerary with Summer.

"We need to be in the East Room at 4:00. At 4:20, you will meet with Mrs. Weatherby, and at 4:30 you will join the rest of the speakers on the dais," Ted explained.

"Will you be up there with me?"

"I can make it happen if you'd like."

"I would like."

"Did they tell you about the sculpture?" Ted asked.

"Yes, something about an eternal flame."

"Right. Well, you will be lighting that flame after you finish your speech," Ted said.

"Oh, my God! My speech! I completely forgot about that. I don't have a speech," Summer said in a panic.

"Yes, you do," Ted said as he pulled it from his pocket. "You should sit down and read it. If you want to make changes, we need to do that now."

Summer parted her lips to speak, but nothing came out. She sat at the kitchen table and unfolded the two sheets of paper with Ted's impeccable handwriting. She began to read. Ted watched her reaction. She was only a couple of paragraphs into the speech when she put her hand up to her mouth and gasped.

She stopped reading and looked at Ted. "This is everything I told you this morning."

"Is that all right? Did I overstep?" he asked, nervously.

Summer reached out and touched Ted's arm. She shook her head. "No. You didn't."

Summer continued reading in silence. Ted took in her gasps and sighs, and he watched her nod. Then she teared up. When finished reading, she stood and wrapped her arms around Ted. Ted returned the warm hug.

"It's perfect," she said. "How did you manage this?"

"I had a lot of help," Ted replied. "Here," he picked up her purse and handed it to her. "I'll tell you on the way."

SUMMER

A parking spot close to the East Room had been reserved for Summer. Ted had made sure of it. They arrived a little early so Summer could freshen up in the restroom.

At four, Ted led Summer into a room where three couples sat.

Ted said, "Summer, these are the first three couples on the clinic's waiting list. They wanted to meet you."

Each couple introduced themselves and spoke of their struggles with conceiving a child. For twenty minutes, they conversed honestly and easily.

"We've used all our savings and have come so close," thirty-two-year-old Missy Anderson said, "but we can't afford the fees anymore. Peter and I both come from large families. To have a family of our own is all we've ever wanted."

"These wonderful doctors are going to do everything they can for you, all of you," Summer said as she looked earnestly at each of them. "Continue to be positive about the process, that's the key." Her heart filled with the desire to help them. She saw herself and Arnold in each of the couples and wished she had a magic wand to wave over them to grant them what they most sincerely wanted.

When Grace Weatherby entered the room, assistants ushered the couples out.

Summer turned to Ted and frowned. "But I want to speak more with them."

"You will," he promised.

"How did you manage this?" Summer asked.

"It was Marci's idea. I just made a phone call." He paused, then added, "Well, I may have presented Grace with an ultimatum," Ted grinned.

"Summer, I am honored to finally meet you face to face. I am Grace Weatherby. I assume Theodore has filled you in on the itinerary."

Offering Ted a sly smile, Summer then stood straight and rigid before saying, "Yes, thank you. Theodore has been a great help."

Grace Weatherby seemed pretentious and condescending, exactly as Summer had imagined after speaking with her several times on the telephone. Summer had repeatedly declined the invitation to attend the grand opening until the fourth phone call when Grace said they had important paperwork for her to sign before they could open the doors. Once Summer agreed and without further consulting her, Grace made arrangements for Summer to speak. Summer's lawyer was tasked with giving her that news. *Sometimes first impressions are spot on*, Summer thought.

"How lovely," Grace responded. "The only thing we haven't quite worked out is getting you to the sculpture to light the eternal flame. Will you need assistance?"

Summer felt a swell of irritation. "Yes, honey, I will. Theodore will be assisting me. He is quite steady on his feet, you know. And a marvelous dancer."

Ted rolled his eyes discreetly but smiled faintly. Then he responded, "I will need to be on the dais with Summer. To assist her," Ted exaggerated the word assist.

Summer nodded.

"All right. I'll have them place an extra chair. Would you mind sitting behind her?" Grace asked Ted.

"That will be satisfactory, yes," he replied.

"All right. There will be a box of fireplace matches at the base of the sculpture for you to light the flame," Grace said.

"That won't be necessary," Ted replied. "Summer has brought her own lighter."

Still smiling, Summer glanced in Ted's direction and dropped her brows. He winked back.

"Okay, then. There will be two speakers before you. Then I will introduce you. After you speak, Theodore will escort you to the sculpture where you will light the eternal flame in honor of your husband. We will snap a few photographs, and then the ceremony will officially be over," Grace explained. "Do you have any questions?"

Summer turned to Ted. "Did you get all of that, Theodore? I'm not sure I will remember it."

Ted cleared his throat, then responded, "Yes, Summer. I've got all that."

When Grace left the room, Summer and Ted no longer held back their amusement.

"You are incorrigible," Ted said.

"How old does she think I am, anyway?" Summer asked, sounding insulted. Then she said, "Oh, Ted. I would've liked to talk with those couples longer."

"Here is what you are going to do. When you get up to speak, look for those three couples. They will be seated in the front row. I want you to read this speech to them." Ted held up the paper. "Talk to them just as if you were still back in this room. All right?"

Summer nodded. "All right."

"How are you holding up?" he asked.

"Surprisingly well. I can't begin to thank you for every . . ."

Just then, a stranger opened the door and said, "It's time."

Summer began to move but Ted stopped her. He looked into her eyes and said, "You are an amazing woman, Summer. If all those people out there knew you like I do, they would feel the same. And you look beautiful."

Ted took Summer by the arm and led her to the dais, up the stairs, and to her seat. Then he took a seat behind her. He never saw the tears he had summoned.

The first two speakers included the governor of Massachusetts and the chairman of Harvard Medical, each with an agenda well beyond helping childless couples. When Grace rose to introduce her, Summer felt Ted's hand on her shoulder.

He leaned in and whispered, "The front row."

LIGHTING THE WAY

SUMMER

Summer didn't notice the resounding applause. Hanging on to the text of her speech with sweat-covered palms, she felt unsteady on her feet as she shuffled her way to the podium. She couldn't help but scan the crowd of a hundred or more people. All went quiet, and Summer stood, gazing down at her peacock blue pumps.

The front row. She heard Ted in her head. Summer lifted her eyes and found the three couples smiling up at her. Then, to her surprise, sitting behind them she saw Marci, Frank, Frankie Jr., and Casey.

Son of a bucket, she thought. She straightened her posture, held her chin high, and began to read.

"Good afternoon. Forty-one years ago, my husband and I experienced the first of three miscarriages."

Summer swallowed hard, then continued.

"Having children was our greatest dream. At enormous expense, we made use of every medical and homeopathic treatment available, but it wasn't meant to be. Over the years, Arnold and I met many couples who shared our dream."

Summer then focused on each of the three couples.

"Some rejoiced in their outcome, others did not. But all of us had the means to at least try."

She paused for effect, looked out at the audience, and slightly raised her voice.

"I don't believe having a child should be exclusive to those with a hefty bank account. There are too many childless couples in need of help, and that is why we are here today."

Summer had to pause as the crowd applauded.

"This cutting edge facility will provide hope to couples of all income levels, religions, ethnicities, and sexual orientation with compassion, care, and innovative technology."

Summer read about new medical technology and how the scientific progress of the nation's researchers put them on the cusp of great innovation. She spoke of community and caring, understanding and overachieving, and an obligation to treat everyone with the utmost respect.

"We should not live in a world where having a child depends on how much money you have, where you live, or who you live with. No." She slapped her hand on the podium, causing feedback from the microphone. "The ability to have a child should not require an abundance of money but only an abundance of love. Thank you."

Summer turned and walked back to her chair. Everyone on the dais stood and clapped. She eyed Ted, and he nudged his head for her to turn around.

The audience were all on their feet, cheering and clapping. Summer gave them a wave and a flick of her hand.

Ted took Summer by the arm, and the two walked to the base of the sculpture hidden beneath a large white canvas.

Grace Weatherby stood at the podium and announced, "Ladies and gentlemen, may I present to you, in honor of Arnold Case, the eternal flame of our new fertility clinic, The Summer House."

A crane lifted the canvas to reveal a twenty-foot sculpture of a hand lighting a candle.

Once more, the crowd burst into applause.

A removable stairway led to the eternal flame.

Summer recalled Grace had mentioned something about matches and spotted them sitting on one the stairway steps. She was about to reach for them when Ted produced a long-handled gold lighter that he had been hiding in the inside pocket of his suit jacket.

Summer gasped when she saw it. "How did you . . . where did you get it?"

Ted replied, "I remembered a story I read about Arnold receiving this gold lighter as an award for his charitable contributions to children's organizations. 'A symbol of lighting the way for children,' the article said. I found out the lighter was still on display at Case Candle, so I called them and explained what was happening today. Don't worry, I made sure it worked. And I promised to bring it back tomorrow," Ted chuckled.

Summer's eyes welled, and her hand trembled.

"Son of a bitch! How do you expect me to climb these stairs now?"

Ted smiled as he handed her the lighter. "I'll be right behind you."

As promised, Ted followed Summer up the stairs, hanging back far enough to stay out of any photographs.

Summer paused at the top of the stairs and whispered something. Then she lit the flame.

Again, the spectators erupted in applause.

TED

Summer turned, handed the lighter down to Ted, and descended the stairs. Ted backed his way down so he could watch her.

Summer reached the bottom of the stairs. Ted was about to take her arm when people engulfed her. He caught a glimpse of her between the bodies, and she did not look comfortable.

He plowed his way through the crowd, repeating, "Excuse me, excuse me," until he reached her and put his arm around her.

"Do you want to get away from here or do you want to stay?" he whispered in her ear.

"Please, get me out of here," she replied.

"I'm sorry," Ted said loudly, looking at his watch, "Summer has another engagement. I really need to keep her on schedule."

Until the crowd around her dispersed, Summer pouted as if to indicate she did not wish to be whisked away.

As they scurried, Summer asked, "Can we just keep going?"

"If that's what you would like, yes, we can," Ted replied.

Summer suddenly stopped walking and sighed. "No, we can't. I'm supposed to sign some papers," she frowned.

"Grace lied about the papers," Ted said.

"What?"

"She lied. She promised everyone she would get you here, and when you repeatedly told her you weren't interested, she panicked and made up the story about signing papers."

"Why that . . ."

"Hi, Summer," Casey yelled as he ran toward her.

Summer turned and saw Casey just as he crashed into her and wrapped his arms around her waist. She hugged him back.

"Easy there, buddy," Ted said, reaching for Summer to steady her.

"It's all right, Ted," Summer laughed as Ted's family approached. "I don't mind being bombarded by this crowd."

She hugged Marci and Frank and stuck her hand out to shake Frankie Jr.'s. He took her hand, looked her in the eyes and said, "That was a great speech, Summer."

"Thank you, Frankie. I understand your father had something to do with that." Summer smiled at Frank.

Frank responded, "But you added a little of your own at the end there. When you hit that podium, the whole place jumped. You had their attention from beginning to end. Truly impressive, Summer."

"How in the world will I ever thank all of you for what you have done for me today?"

"You could make us some chocolate chip pancakes," Casey said.

"It's a deal," Summer laughed. "Now, since I don't have papers to sign, can we please get the heck out of here?"

"Okay, we'll meet you there," Ted said to Frank.

Frank nodded, and he, Marci, and the boys walked toward the parking lot.

"You have a wonderful family, Ted," Summer said.

"I have to agree with you there. Are you ready?"

Summer gave Ted a weary look as he opened the car door for her. "Absolutely. I just want to put my feet up and relax with a nice glass of wine."

"Uh oh," Ted said.

"Uh oh?" Summer questioned, nestling into the soft leather seat.

"I just thought, after all the anxiety you had about today . . . well, I made reservations at Toscano. Marci and Frank are meeting us there. But, if you'd rather not I can call and cancel the reservations. Marci and the gang can come to the house, and we can get takeout or something." Ted was about to close the passenger door when Summer began to cry.

"Hey," Ted continued, "I'm sorry. I didn't mean to upset you."

Summer wiped her eyes and shook her head. "You didn't upset me. I can't believe I'm crying. It's so ridiculous."

"What is it?" Ted asked with a concerned expression.

"I don't know. I'm not usually a crier. It's just that you and your family have been so incredibly nice. You've handled every single detail, even dinner." Summer threw her hands up. "I never could have gotten through today without you. I don't know," Summer said, shaking her head again. "I guess I was a little more anxious than I thought, and it's all coming out now. I feel like an idiot."

Ted reached into his suit jacket pocket, produced a handkerchief, and handed it to Summer.

Summer sobbed louder. Holding up the handkerchief, she spouted, "See what I mean? Every detail."

Ted chuckled, knelt, put his hand on her knee, and said, "You're not an idiot, you're just letting out a lot of stress." Ted stood, closed her door, and got in the driver's seat.

Summer dried her eyes. "I'm sorry," she said. "I don't know what got into me."

"There's nothing to be sorry about. This was a tough day. And you were a trooper. I'll take you back to the house."

"No." Summer shouted. "I want to go to Toscano with you and your family."

Ted smiled. "Well, all right then," he said as he pressed the car's push button starter.

Summer finished dabbing her eyes, then let out a light laugh. "You're not going to tell them about my breakdown, are you?"

"It depends on how much wine we have," he grinned.

><><

Ted had reserved a table for seven.

"Why the extra setting, Dad?" Marci asked.

"I invited Dan. He said he would try to make it," Ted replied just as he saw Dan walk through the door. "Speaking of . . . there he is."

The maître d' escorted Dan to their table. Ted stood to shake his hand and said, "Dan, I'd like you to meet Summer. Summer, this is Dr. Dan Parsons, the third member of your speech-writing team."

"It's very nice to meet you, Summer," Dan said.

"And you, Doctor Parsons. I can't thank you enough for your

help with the speech. You all made me sound like I knew what I was talking about," Summer chuckled.

"You can thank me by calling me Dan. So, how did it go? I wish I could have been there," Dan said as he took the empty chair across from Summer.

"She was a big hit," Ted answered.

"She was sensational," Frank echoed.

"You should have seen it when she pounded the desk," Casey said.

Everyone laughed.

"The podium, Casey. And Summer didn't pound it, she . . . okay, maybe she pounded it," Marci capitulated.

"I don't know what made me do that," Summer laughed.

"It had great effect visually if not audibly," said Ted.

Ted ordered two bottles of Prosecco for the table as conversation took flight.

After an array of Italian entrées followed by shared desserts, they sipped coffee.

Dan asked Summer, "So, what now? Where do you go from here?"

"Back to my quiet little campsite in New York until I figure out what's next," Summer replied.

"And you, Ted?" Dan asked.

"Yes, I'm heading back there. too."

"For how long?" Dan persisted.

"Ah, I don't know. I haven't thought about it."

The fact that he hadn't thought about his future at all suddenly struck Ted as odd.

"That's quite a hurdle you've jumped," Dan said.

"What do you mean?"

"For as long as I've known you, you've known exactly what your next step would be," Dan replied.

"I'd call that progress," Summer said.

I'd call that unsettling, Ted thought.

⁓

Ted hadn't spoken during the drive to his home.

"You're awfully quiet," Summer said. "Is everything okay?"

Ted paused, then replied with a thin smile, "Yes, everything's fine. I guess I'm just a little tired."

"It's no wonder. It's been a long day."

When they returned to Ted's house, Summer went upstairs to change into pajama's, bathrobe, and slippers.

Ted sat on the couch in front of the gas fireplace sipping whiskey when Summer came back downstairs. His suit coat hung over the back of the couch, and his tie lay on the coffee table. He had removed his shoes and placed them neatly beside the table.

Summer poured herself some whiskey and sat on the other end of the couch with her legs folded beneath her.

"Let's have it," she said.

"What?"

"Something is bothering you. What is it?" she asked.

Ted took a sip of whiskey. "I don't know what I'm doing."

"About what?"

"About anything."

"I don't understand," Summer said.

"I have no idea what I'm going to do tomorrow."

"Sure, you do. We're going to bring the lighter back to Case."

Ted glared at Summer as if she had made a horrible joke at an inopportune time.

"Oh, that's not what you meant, is it?" Summer asked. "Is this about what Dan said? About jumping the hurdle?"

Ted softened his expression. "He made me realize I don't

have a purpose anymore. I don't have any direction, obligation, or contribution to make."

"Well, that's just not true," Summer gently raised her voice. "You have an obligation to your daughter and grandchildren—the biggest and most important kind of obligation."

"Yes, I know that, but I mean, personally. You know, being useful. Being a productive member of society. Dan was right. I've always known exactly what my next step would be. But I don't have a clue anymore. Maybe I made a mistake. Maybe I shouldn't have given up my practice."

"Do you think you were more productive to society when you were working?" Summer asked.

"Yes!"

Summer sighed. "I think it's time we had the talk."

"The talk?"

"Yes, the big one."

"I've already fathered a child, so I think I understand how it works."

"Aren't you clever." Summer flashed a fake smile. "Pour yourself another whiskey, Ted. This could take a while, and debate could become lively."

Ted topped off his and Summer's whiskeys.

Summer asked, "What do you think the meaning of life is?"

"Oh, that is a big one. All right, let me think for a minute."

Ted took a sip and stared into the uniform flames of the fire. After a few moments, he replied, "To always do your best, work hard, and be kind to each other."

"Do you believe in reincarnation?" Summer asked.

"No."

"That's it? No explanation, just no?"

"I believe in being succinct and to the point," Ted answered.

He watched as Summer rolled her eyes.

Then she said, "Okay, here we go. What if I told you that you and I knew each other in a previous life?"

Ted chuckled. "I'd say you had a vivid imagination."

"Well, at least you didn't say I was crazy."

"To be honest, that would have been my first response, but I'm trying to be kind to others."

"Do you believe we all have souls?" Summer asked.

Ted gave it some thought and replied, "Yes, I do."

"Thank the Lord. Okay, what happens to your soul when you die?"

"What happens to it? It dies, I guess."

"But your soul isn't part of your body. It doesn't have physical mass like a heart or lung. If it's not physical, how can it die?"

Ted followed his own logical thinking and said, "It doesn't have a host body anymore. How could it survive?"

"But what if it did? What if the soul goes back to where it originated? Let's call that place heaven."

Ted took another sip of whiskey and thought through what Summer had just said. "Where it originated? Are you saying you think when a child is born, they are inhabited by a soul from heaven? One that was on this earth previously?"

"Not inhabited exactly, but let's leave that discussion for another time. For now, let's use the premise that the soul enters the child at inception," Summer said.

"Okay. Then what?"

"The child lives a full life being tested, learning lessons or not. These lessons stay with the soul. In one life, you may be full of greed. If you don't learn not to be greedy during that lifetime, you are destined to repeat the lesson, maybe tested more aggressively in whatever persona you reincarnate. Do you see what I'm saying?"

"Yes, you're saying that we keep coming back to this earth to learn lessons on what? How to be a good person?"

"Or how to be a perfect soul," Summer said.

"Do you really believe that?"

"I'm simplifying what I believe."

"So, becoming a perfect soul is the meaning of life?"

"No," Summer shook her head. "Becoming a perfect soul is the ultimate outcome. The meaning of life can be summed up in two words."

"Well?" Ted raised his eyebrows in anticipation.

"Unconditional love," Summer said.

"That's it, love?" Ted asked.

"Unconditional."

"That seems too easy. How can that be the meaning of life?"

"You think learning and living unconditional love is easy?" Summer asked. "That means no judgment, no anger, unconditional forgiveness, and service for the betterment of the universe and humanity."

"Well, when you put it that way, no wonder it would take so many lifetimes," Ted chuckled.

"You think I'm crazy, don't you?" Summer asked.

"No. Absolutely not. Who am I to say? It's interesting to think about, though. What you're saying is that the more you learn and the better person you are in this life, the easier the next life will be?"

"Yes, to put it simply. Let me ask you this. Have you ever met someone for the first time who you instantly liked or disliked for no apparent reason?"

Ted found himself thinking of Carol. "Yes, I have."

"I believe that's because you have a history with the soul that person possesses. Your souls are part of your soul family. We incorporate our soul family into each life. Maybe not all of them in each lifetime, but some. We are constantly being tested in big and small ways. Our choices and our actions have consequences."

"Like I said, it's an interesting concept," Ted said.

"Just one more thing," Summer said. "What you, your family, and your friend did for me today was one of the most amazing displays of unconditional love I have ever experienced. So don't for one minute think you are not contributing to the greater good. And I will knock your block off if I ever hear you say you're not useful."

Summer shot back the last of her whiskey, put the glass on the coffee table, and said, "Ponder that big one. I'm exhausted. I'm going to bed. Goodnight, Ted."

"Goodnight, Summer." But she had gone before he was able to get the words out.

SLEEPLESS NIGHTS

SUMMER

As tired as she was, Summer couldn't sleep. Segments of the day played over and over in her head as if she watched them in a movie trailer, Ted's expression when she stood ready to leave for the grand opening, Ted walking her arm-in-arm to the dais, Ted staring up at her as she walked down the stairs after lighting the eternal flame, and Ted sitting on the couch, the firelight flickering between them.

She squeezed her eyes shut to blot out the visions. The more she concentrated on removing Ted from her mind, the more challenging it got. She knew she was in trouble. As hard as she tried to keep from thinking about him, she just couldn't stop.

Summer had deeply and hopelessly fallen in love with Ted. And there was nothing she could do about it. She had made him a promise, a pact, and she couldn't go back on her word. She refused to put Ted in that awkward position.

All these years thinking I would never find love again, and now this. Maybe my example about greed was more apt than I thought. Maybe I am greedy for wanting love twice in one lifetime. "Is that so wrong?" she whispered.

TED

Sipping his morning coffee, Ted sat at the kitchen table reading the *Wall Street Journal* news from his laptop. He looked up when Summer came into the kitchen. "I was getting a little worried," Ted said as he eyed the time—8:15.

"I didn't sleep well last night," she replied.

Ted closed the cover of his laptop and looked concerned.

"Are you all right?"

"Yes, I'm fine. I just think yesterday took its toll on me."

Ted nodded, assuming Summer had been thinking a lot about Arnold and therefore hadn't been able to sleep. "I can understand that. You should take it easy today. Here, sit. I'll get you some coffee."

"Don't you start treating me like an old lady. I had enough of that from that lying Weatherby woman." Summer reached for a cup and poured. "I swear, if Casey hadn't come running up to us at that moment, I might have gone to slap her silly."

"What happened to unconditional love?" Ted laughed.

"Do I look like an enlightened being to you?"

"You look beautiful," Ted blurted. "When you're angry. You look beautiful when you're angry."

Ted lifted the laptop cover as an excuse to avert his eyes.

He didn't know what got into him. *Why did I say that?*

Ted had not slept well, either. He also reviewed the day over and over and how good it felt to be able to do something meaningful for someone he liked very much. Summer continued to awe him with her courage, convictions, and pure heart. Watching her at the podium during her speech had stirred him. And then, thinking back on it as he had tried to sleep had had the same effect.

He had tossed and turned. His brain flipped through memories like a PowerPoint presentation—Summer sipping wine in the vineyard by the lake. Summer twirling in the river. Summer standing in his kitchen, oblivious to her striking appearance. And Summer sitting on his couch, the flames of the fire setting her face aglow.

Ted had conceded that he liked Summer very much. *Dammit, Ted. You made a deal.* Filling the awkward silence, he said, "We never talked about how long we would stay here. I thought maybe we could head back tomorrow. How does that sound?"

"That would be fine. But I would really like to do something nice for all of you before we go. Do you think Marci and Frank would be available to come to dinner tonight?"

"You know that's not necessary, right?"

"Yes, I do. But I'd like to do it. Besides, I promised Casey chocolate chip pancakes."

"I'll give Marci a call."

With dinner plans affirmed, Summer borrowed Ted's secondary car to go grocery shopping. Ted delivered the lighter back to Case Candles, then went to his former office to pick up the few things he had left behind and have a short visit with Chip.

"How's Summer?" Chip asked.

"She's good. The grand opening went well."

"Have you two, you know—are you an item yet?"

"No. Is that all you ever think about, Chip?"

Chip gave Ted a backhand to his shoulder. With one eyebrow lifted, he replied, "Pretty much. What are you waiting for? She's terrific. And I saw how you two are together."

Ted's eyebrows furrowed. "What do you mean, how we are together?"

"Come on, Ted. You're a grown man. You must feel the chemistry."

"Sorry, Chip. You got it wrong this time. Neither one of us is looking for that."

"Tell yourself what you will, buddy, but I never get it wrong."

As he drove home, Ted thought about Chip's comments. They reminded him he should remain cognizant of his actions and expressions when he was with Summer. He did not wish to put her in an awkward position, no matter his feelings. He had made her a promise, and he intended to keep it.

Ted turned onto the highway. Alone in the car, he let his guard down and allowed himself to examine his feelings for Summer.

She makes me laugh. I like listening to her stories, thoughts, and theories. I enjoy doing things for her. Ted smiled.

She's smart, sincere, and silly. He chuckled, picturing her jumping on the bed. *And she's independent and self-sufficient.*

I can't imagine a day going by without seeing her.

Ted's eyes widened.

"Son of a . . . . I might be in love with Summer," he said aloud as he drove by his exit. The remainder of Ted's afternoon was filled with anxiety, confusion, and outright fear.

❧ ❧

For dinner, Summer made her version of Beef Wellington—beef tenderloin coated with wild mushroom paté, encased in puff pastry, and roasted to a perfect medium rare. She drizzled the beef with a Merlot-reduced demi-glace and served with creamed pearl onions, steamed broccoli rabe, and rosemary-roasted potatoes.

She had also prepared chocolate chip pancakes for Casey, which he opted to eat instead of beef.

The conversation was lively. Summer spent most of dinner talking with Marci and Frank while Ted engaged in banter with the boys.

"That was an amazing meal. Thank you, Summer," Marci said as she placed her hand on her stomach.

"It's one of the best meals I've ever had," Frank said, then winked at his wife. "Sorry, honey."

"Yes, you will pay for that remark," Marci joked.

"Yeah, it was great," said Frankie Jr.

"I bet the pancakes were better, Frankie," Casey grinned with a chocolate-covered mouth.

"Well, thank you. I love cooking for all of you," Summer replied.

After coffee and a slice of lemon meringue pie, Summer kicked them out of the dining room and kitchen, insisting on cleaning up herself. Frank took the boys to the basement to play pool, leaving Marci alone with Ted in the living room.

"What's going on, Dad?" Marci asked.

"With what?"

"With you and Summer."

Ted looked at Marci with a grimace. "Nothing. I'm not sure what you're getting at."

"You hardly looked at her during dinner. You didn't talk to her and never complimented or thanked her for the meal."

"What are you talking about? We were all talking. Every one of us. It was nice. I'll thank her for dinner. I just forgot."

"I'm not a fool, Dad. I've seen how the two of you *are* together."

What is with everybody? Ted thought with frustration. He didn't know how to respond without sounding defensive.

"Something's wrong with both of you," Marci continued. She glared at Ted.

"Look, Marci, I like Summer. I like her a lot. But what you think is happening between us can never happen."

"Why not?"

"It just can't, that's all," Ted said defiantly.

"The two of you are crazy about each other. It's so damned obvious. Why would you say it can't happen?" Marci demanded.

"Don't swear." He paused. "You'll just have to trust me. It's not going to happen."

"Your being stubborn, Dad. You won't even consider the possibility?"

"Look, Marci," Ted said, careful not to be overheard. "It won't happen because we made a pact weeks ago that it wouldn't happen." He thought how strange that must sound.

"You did what?" Marci screamed.

Summer yelled from the kitchen. "Are you talking to me, Marci?"

Ted's eyes bulged as he glanced toward the kitchen.

"Yes," Ted yelled. "Marci and I are going for a little walk to burn off dinner. We'll be back soon."

He grabbed Marci by the arm and guided her to the front door.

"Okay. Enjoy yourselves," Summer yelled back.

Ted held up his index finger, indicating that Marci should wait before speaking again.

The setting sun left an amber glow on the horizon. Most of the neighbors were already home with shades drawn and well into their nightly routines. Ted held Marci around the waist, steering her down the driveway to the sidewalk. Once they turned the corner beyond the neighbors' high hedges, he stopped and turned to face her.

Marci spurted. "You made a pact? Who the hell makes a pact not to fall in love?"

"Keep your voice down. The neighbors don't need a show. Look, I know it sounds . . . odd, but at the time, it made perfect sense."

"In whose world does that make sense?"

Ted lowered his head, rubbed his forehead with his hand, and sighed. "In the world of a man scared to death he will dishonor his dead wife's memory. In the world of a man who hasn't been with any other woman in over forty years and in the world of a man who is just . . . afraid to open his heart again."

Marci started to speak, but nothing came out.

Ted noticed a tear form in the corner of her eye and wiped it away with his thumb.

"Dad, I'm so sorry. I didn't realize you felt that way. I should have. I'm such an idiot," Marci said.

"Hey, stop that. You are no such thing. You just worry about me, and I appreciate that, even if I do give you a hard time about it," Ted chuckled.

She reached for her father and hugged him. He wrapped his arms around her and laid his head on top of hers.

"Your father is a mess, pumpkin."

"No, my father is the most wonderful human being on this earth," she replied. Releasing their hug, she said, "You know Mom would want you to be happy."

"I do."

"And I want you to be happy. And Summer makes you happy."

"She does. But I can't break my promise to her. It wouldn't be fair to put her in that position."

"Wait. Are you telling me this pact thing was Summer's idea?" Marci asked.

"Yes."

"That doesn't make sense."

"If it isn't what she wanted, she would not have suggested it. I have to respect that," Ted said. "And so do you."

Ted and Marci walked arm in arm for a while before turning back toward the house.

"What are you going to do?" Marci asked.

"I am going to enjoy spending time with my very good friend."

"Oh, Dad," Marci whimpered, holding her hand over her heart. Then she kissed him on the cheek. When they returned to the house, Marci went straight to the kitchen.

MARCI

"Summer, you just have to let me help you finish up in here. Besides, you're leaving tomorrow. It will give us a chance to talk."

"All right." Summer handed Marci a dishcloth. "I haven't wiped down the counter yet. Did you have a nice walk?"

"We did. Dad seems so much more relaxed these days." Marci began cleaning. "Thank you again for dinner. It was amazing. Did you see how Dad devoured it?" she asked.

Summer smiled. "I love cooking for your father. He's such a voracious eater. And there's not much that he doesn't like. He hasn't even realized he's eating healthier."

"The two of you have gotten pretty close, huh?"

Summer paused, then replied, "About as close as two friends can be, I guess."

Marci frowned. "Oh, I guess I hoped maybe you had become more than friends."

"Oh, honey. When a person has had true love in their life, sometimes it's enough. But we can never have too many good friends."

Shortly after, as Marci prepared to leave, she hugged her father fiercely. "I love you, Dad."

Ted sensed a sadness in Marci's hug. "I love you, too, pumpkin. Don't you worry about me. I'm going to be just fine."

OUT OF SIGHT

SUMMER

Halfway back to Sunset Pines Campground and without preamble, Ted asked Summer, "What happens to the soul when it has achieved perfection?"

Surprised that Ted had been thinking about their conversation from two nights prior, Summer responded, "Ascension. There's no longer a need to inhabit the earth. The soul then lives in the light of love or what you may call God."

"Okay, that's way over my head, and I don't want you to explain it to me. But you are saying that perfection is achievable."

"Yes, it is achievable," Summer grinned. "Now I understand why that concept appeals to you, Mr. Perfection."

Ted chuckled. "Hardly."

"But you try. That's the point. All we can do is our best."

"So my father was right all those times he preached perfection?" Ted blurted.

"Well, wait a minute now. You told me your father's idea of perfection was telling you how to think, feel, speak, and live. That's not perfection. That's a dictatorship. Now, if he taught you how to love, forgive, and have compassion for others, which he must have because you have all those attributes, that's the kind of perfection we should strive for."

"No, my father didn't teach us those things, but my mother did," Ted responded.

"Well, then. Your mother is a beautiful soul," Summer praised. "You've been stewing on this, haven't you?"

"Only a little."

She wasn't convinced and glanced at him.

"Okay, maybe a little more than a little."

"Ted, you're not your father. And you were never obligated to become him. But I get it. It's difficult to let go of those expectations. If you want my opinion . . ." She stopped to wait for his approval to continue.

Ted nodded.

"I believe you chose your father for this lifetime so you could learn to think for yourself, stand up to your ideals, and hold on to your convictions not in spite of the difficulty but because of it. The challenge netted you growth, and I'd say you knocked it out of the park."

Ted shook his head. "Wait. I chose my father?"

"Oh, boy. I didn't intend to go that deep, but yes. I believe we choose our life's lessons and the souls we surround ourselves with before we reincarnate."

"That's it. My head is going to explode," Ted said.

Summer laughed. "Well, I did warn you."

They engaged in sparse conversation for the rest of the trip. Summer could tell Ted ruminated on their discussion, and she did not wish to disturb him. The fact that he would even discuss the subject only endeared him to her more, which in turn made her feel more dishonest about hiding her true feelings. But revealing them did not coincide with her goal of becoming enlightened.

Back at the campground, Summer and Ted went their separate ways, Summer to unload her suitcase, Ted to unload everything he brought from home to fully stock his motorhome.

There was no campfire or dinner that night. Summer and Ted waved to each other the following morning, but Ted did not join the line for dinner that evening.

Summer continued feeding the campers, but Ted only sporadically showed up with a plate, and when he did, they merely exchanged pleasantries. They shared short conversations over the course of the next week but kept them simple and not personal. Ted always put money in the coffee can, then took the food back to his trailer. It was all very neighborly but agonizing for Summer.

The next week one late afternoon, a delivery truck pulled up to Summer's campsite and left a package on her doorstep. She knew she had not ordered anything and checked the label to see who the package belonged to. It read Theodore Winter.

Summer primped her hair and brushed her cheeks with blush before carrying the package across the lane. She knocked three times on the door.

"Summer, hello," Ted said, wearing a smile and the unicorn t-shirt Summer had bought him.

Summer pointed at the shirt and laughed. "I can't believe you are wearing it. Oh, here," she handed Ted the package. "This was delivered to me by mistake."

"Thank you," Ted said, then tentatively added, "Do you want to come in for coffee or something?"

Just as tentatively, Summer replied, "Yes, that would be nice."

She stepped up into the motorhome and glanced around.

"It looks like you finally have everything you need," she said.

"Yes, I think so," he replied.

"So, then, what's in the box?" Summer asked before saying, "I'm sorry. I didn't mean to be nosey."

Ted smiled an awkward, boyish, self-conscious smile. "Not at all," he said as he opened the box. He removed two books, both of which Summer was familiar with.

"Ted, you're reading about reincarnation?"

"I've been researching it online, and these are supposed to be very good books on the subject."

"They are. I could have loaned them to you," Summer chuckled.

"Have a seat. I was thinking about opening a bottle of wine. Would you join me if I did?"

"I could be convinced."

"Great." Ted turned first one way, then the other before reaching for a bottle of wine.

Absent-mindedly wringing her hands, Summer sat in the recliner.

"How have you been?" Ted asked.

"Good. And you?"

"Good. Yes."

Ted poured two glasses from a bottle of Cabernet and handed one to Summer. When their eyes met, she felt warm all over.

"It's good to see you," he smiled.

"You, too." Summer effortlessly returned the smile.

"What have you been up to?" Ted asked.

"My usual. Meditating, cooking, and a little reading. How about you?"

"Thinking, mostly, I guess."

"Apparently," Summer said, eyeing the two books. "Have you spoken with Marci lately? How is the family?"

"They're good. I spoke with her this morning. She wanted me to say hello to you."

"That's nice," Summer smiled.

An uncomfortable silence followed, each taking sips of their wine. Ted still stood in front of Summer.

Ted finally stammered, "I . . . uh, I've . . . missed you, hanging out with you, I mean."

Summer looked down at her hands and sighed. "I've missed you, too. You know, hanging out."

"Maybe we should do something. Plan a day or something."

"All right. What should we do?"

"I don't know. Whatever you would like to do," Ted answered.

"I've got an idea," Summer said. "Why don't you pick something you would like to do, and I'll pick something I would like to do, and we'll do both."

"What if we both pick the same thing?"

"Then we'll do it twice as long," Summer replied, wishing it possible that her first choice would indeed be his.

"Tomorrow?"

"Tomorrow."

"Okay," Ted grinned and sat down.

Ted filled Summer in on Marci, Frank, and the boys. Summer told Ted about the authors of the books he was about to read. They talked and laughed until it was time for Summer to get ready to serve dinner.

"Are you coming for dinner tonight?" she asked.

"I'll be there."

That night after dinner, Summer sat outside her camper on her meditating mat. Crickets filled the silence. She thought about how she wished to spend her time with Ted the next day, but images from her dreams kept creeping into her brain, images she could never share with him.

She had tried to discourage her feelings for Ted. She avoided him when possible and filled her head with nonsensical reasons why they should not be together.

"Fudgemouth!" she cried. *Why did I ever suggest that ridiculous pact?*

Summer thought she heard a thump coming from Ted's trailer. She listened but heard nothing more.

I don't think I can bear this anymore. There's only one thing left to do. I need to leave, Summer thought. *We'll spend one last day together tomorrow, but then I have to leave. I'll head to Ohio.*

TED

Ted sat at his kitchen table after dinner that night with a pad of paper and pen to write a list of things he would like to do with Summer—none of which were suitable for her to see.

He had thought the longer he stayed away from her, the less he would want her. But the opposite had occurred. He could not stop thinking about her.

"Dammit!" Ted pounded the table and the sound echoed off the walls. *Why did I agree to that insane pact?*

Come morning, Ted's stomach jittered. He'd found a few activities that he thought Summer would enjoy, but he was so anxious about their outing that he began to wonder why he suggested it in the first place. He supposed he did it to determine whether he could be satisfied being just friends with Summer.

It was nine when he stepped outside to see Summer finishing up her meditation. They walked toward each other and met in the middle of the lane.

"Good morning," said Ted.

"Good morning. You're wearing a suit."

"I wasn't sure what to plan for, so I thought this could cover most anything. I packed a small bag of clothing just in case."

Summer chuckled. "Not long ago, you showed up here with that huge vehicle and almost nothing else. Now you are packing a day bag as a contingency plan. I'd say you have come full circle with this retirement thing, Ted."

"If I've learned anything from hanging around with you, it's to expect the unexpected. So, what have you come up with?" Ted asked.

"I could not think of one specific thing I wanted to do. I would be happy if we just hop in the car and see what happens. Did you come up with anything?" Summer asked.

"Well, I did some research—"

"Of course, you did," Summer smirked.

Ted eyed her mockingly, then continued, "I found a farmers' market that looks like it could be fun. It's a bit of a drive, though."

"Sounds great. Do you want to drive, or shall I?" Summer asked.

"I'll drive. I already packed some things in the car."

"I just need to get a few things from the camper. I'll meet you in the car," Summer said.

It was a perfect spring morning with the temperature expected to reach the high seventies. Ted headed south, skirting Cayuga Lake. The wineries prepared for the increased tourist activity, evident by multiple tour buses they passed along the way.

"Now that's a smart way to tour the wineries, don't you think?" Summer asked.

"Only if you want to be stuck on a bus with a talkative, drunk, loud-mouthed individual." Ted caught Summer's frown in response to his reply. "Trust me. There's one on every bus."

"And you know this from experience?"

"I do. When we were young, Carol and I couldn't afford a reliable car, so we took bus tours to a casino, wineries, and once to a football game. It never failed. Every time there was at least one person—man or woman—who didn't understand the concept of personal space."

"I could never get Arnold to do a bus tour. I wanted to do one in London so we could easily visit all the tourist spots. Instead, we almost died multiple times when Arnold forgot to drive on the left side of the road. We spent most of our time looking for parking, then got fined for not paying a congestion charge. So we never got to stop anywhere. We just drove past everything."

Ted chuckled. "I think I would have liked Arnold very much."

"Oh, I have no doubt."

"Did you travel much?" Ted asked.

"Not really. He didn't like to be away from work. And I worked most weekends in the early days. But we found ways to get away locally to decompress."

"Carol always wanted to go to London. We figured we would go when we retired," Ted said solemnly. "If there is one thing I wish I had learned earlier in life, that would be it."

"What would?"

"Not to wait for the perfect time to do the things you want to do because there is no guarantee that you will be here for it."

"Absolutely."

They stopped for coffee and bagels at a small family-owned restaurant and farm stand.

Sitting at an outdoor table as they watched the sun crest the distant trees, Summer asked, "What's the craziest thing you ever did?"

"Oh, no. You're not getting any dirt on me."

"Dirt? On you? I bet you never did one crazy or dangerous thing in your life."

"And you would be wrong."

"Then tell me."

"No, I don't think I will. I can't have my daughter finding out about my sordid past."

"You would be surprised at the secrets I can keep," Summer said.

"You first."

Summer took a sip of coffee, then grinned. "I got arrested for being a Peeping Tom."

"Wow. I didn't see that one coming. Who were you peeping at?" Ted asked.

"I didn't say I was peeping. I said I got arrested for peeping."

"Okay, what happened?"

"You see, there were these monkeys."

Ted spit a mouthful of his coffee onto his shoe. "Monkeys?"

Summer laughed and handed him a napkin. "Yes, monkeys. I was seventeen years old and had a friend who attended the local college. She told me that the school was using monkeys for research. Well, I had to do something about that, didn't I? So, my friend and I stole a ladder from the maintenance building. My plan was to go into the lab after hours through an open window on the second floor and release the monkeys. Unbeknownst to me, the open window was in the women's bathroom, just off the laboratory, and a female upperclassman happened to be using it at the time."

Ted howled. "And you climbed in the window?"

"No, I didn't get the chance. The girl screamed and security came running. She reported a Peeping Tom, and the rest is self-explanatory."

"And you got arrested," Ted said, snorting through the sentence.

"Yes. But then I explained that I wasn't peeping, I was merely breaking and entering to free the monkeys. The local police found it hysterical and let me go."

"That's a great story. Except for the poor monkeys," Ted said.

"Well, that's the funny thing. There were never any monkeys. Apparently, my friend was very gullible."

Ted laughed heartily, then remarked, "I would have liked to have seen seventeen-year-old Summer on her quest to save the monkeys."

"I would like to be that girl again," Summer mused.

"Would you? Really? If given the chance, would you go back to that time?" Ted asked.

"Oh, I don't know. I suppose not. I like the person I am now."

I do, too, Ted thought.

Summer continued, "Your turn."

"Well, my story isn't as exciting as yours. We were in our mid-twenties, and Carol and I . . . wait, you won't repeat this to anyone, right?"

"I promise." Summer crossed her heart with her index finger like she had when promising something as a young girl.

"Carol and I went skinny dipping," Ted said.

"Come on, Ted. That's nothing. I did that last summer for crying out loud."

Ted arched his eyebrow as he pictured Summer naked, swimming in a stream. Then he continued. "You didn't let me finish. We went skinny dipping in the mayor's built-in swimming pool, which was surrounded by a locked gate, which we climbed over while the mayor and his wife slept."

"Why, Ted Winter, you do have an adventurous streak in you, no pun intended. What happened? Did you get away with it?"

"Barely. We got a little carried away in the swimming pool, and Carol shrieked. When we saw the bedroom lights turn on, we high-tailed it out of there."

Summer cackled. "I sure hope they cleaned that pool before they used it again."

Ted shot her a mischievous glance.

Back on the road, Summer found a classic rock radio station, and they sang their way to the southern end of Cayuga Lake. The sun sat high in the sky by the time they pulled into the farmers' market parking lot.

The main building housed permanent businesses, including a flower shop, glass-blowing artisan, bakery, and Case Candle outlet.

"Look at that," Ted said, amused. "Did you know this was here?"

"I knew we had an outlet somewhere around the area, but I didn't know it was here. It's quite cute, isn't it? But it's not mine to worry about anymore," Summer smiled.

Beyond the main building, a gravel walkway extended. Pop-up tents lined each side. Vendors sold produce, jams, crafts, and clothing. There were wine tastings, beer samplings, ice cream cones, and cheese.

They spent hours strolling the market. Summer bought cheese and produce, and Ted bought jam.

"I could use a break. Let's find someplace to sit," Summer said.

To their left was a double-wide tent with white plastic tables and folding chairs. Toward the back of the tent stood a small wine bar. When they approached the podium at the front of the tent, they noticed a sign which read Birdhouse & Blush $20.

Ted inquired about the sign.

The woman manning the podium told them that for twenty dollars, they could have a glass of blush wine and build and paint a birdhouse to take home with them.

"What do you think?" Ted asked Summer.

"I love it. Let's do it."

FACING THE MUSIC

SUMMER

Summer and Ted sat at a table. An attendant brought each a glass of wine and a box that held everything they needed to build and paint their birdhouses.

The birdhouse parts were cut to size, and the box included directions, wood glue, and clamps to put the parts together. When assembled, they resembled a small house with a hole in front for birds to enter and a perch for them to sit upon.

They helped each other hold the pieces steady while the other glued and clamped them together. While the glue dried, they sipped wine and spoke easily. They laughed at their clumsiness and marveled at their accomplishments.

The paint palettes were limited but sufficient. Summer painted her birdhouse white and covered it with colorful flowers, using purple, orange, red, and yellow.

Ted painted his birdhouse with a red front and sides and a white roof.

The final piece was to insert a screw eye with an attached chain to hang the house.

"I'd say we did pretty well," Ted said, admiring both houses.

"I can't wait to hang it at the camp . . . site." Summer stuttered as she remembered her plan to leave the next day for Ohio.

"It's going to look great," Ted said. "Mine is going to hang from the pine tree on the back side of my site. Somebody here must sell birdseed, right?"

Summer could only produce a light smile and nod.

Ted seemed the happiest Summer had seen him since they returned to New York. They strolled and found a vendor who sold birdhouses, and Ted purchased a bag of seeds.

"I'm hungry. Are you hungry?" he asked, smiling like a child.

Unable to resist the smile, Summer chuckled. "Yes, I'm hungry."

"Why don't we try that winery we passed about a half hour from here? It looked like they had outdoor dining," Ted suggested.

"That sounds great," Summer replied, desperately trying to hide the fact that her heart ached. She scolded herself. She vowed then not to let her emotions ruin the wonderful day.

They shared an early dinner while sitting on the porch of a castle overlooking the lake. The sun sat low in the sky but did not rush to sink below the horizon.

Over coffee, Ted pulled a sheet of paper from his pocket and said, "I picked up the schedule of events from the birdhouse place. Next week is Burgundy & Basket Weaving. What do you say?"

Summer experienced a sharp pain and placed her hand on her chest. "Oh," she said.

Ted jumped from his chair and reached his hand across the table. "Are you all right?"

Summer quickly replied, "Yes, I'm fine. Just a little heartburn, that's all," she said as she waved her hand for him to sit.

"Maybe I should get you home?" Ted asked.

"I suppose we should," Summer replied.

The ride was quiet. Ted asked many times during the long drive how she was feeling. Each time, she said, "I'm fine, thank you."

When close to home, Summer said, "This has been a wonderful day. Thank you, Ted."

"I had a great time, too. Thank you. Lucky for us, we can do this again any time we want."

Summer closed her eyes and turned her head to face the window. She hadn't felt heartburn but heartache brought on not from something she ate but from the impossible situation she had created. She had planned on the ride back to the campground to tell Ted she would leave in the morning but found that she couldn't.

Not tonight, she thought. *But I'll have to tell him in the morning.*

Ted parked the SUV in front of his motorhome, got out, and walked around to the passenger side to open Summer's door. She had already begun to get out, but he took her hand as she stood.

He lingered, with her hand in his, staring into her eyes. "Summer?"

"Yes, Ted."

"I . . ." Ted lowered his eyes and let go of her hand, "don't forget your produce."

Summer reached into the car and took hold of the bag. Then she turned and said, "Goodnight. Thank you for a memorable day."

"Goodnight, Summer."

TED

Another near sleepless night. Ted had come close to asking Summer to stay with him. On the drive home, he had labored to find the words. *Summer, I love you. I never thought I could love anyone this much again, but I can't imagine a day going by without seeing and talking to you. Please tell me you feel the same. Stay with me tonight.* But he couldn't get the words out.

So Ted lay in bed, unable to sleep, wondering what her response would have been if he hadn't been such a coward.

Weary eyed, unshaven, and dragging, Ted stepped out of his motorhome that morning to see Summer carrying her gong to the van. On closer inspection, he noticed all of her outdoor furniture gone and her lights taken down. He suddenly felt very much awake.

He ran across the street and caught Summer just as she closed the back doors of her van.

Summer smiled and said, "Oh, good morning, Ted."

"Summer, what are you doing?" Ted asked nervously.

"I'm packing up."

"What for?"

"I'm heading to Ohio," she said matter-of-factly.

"But you can't. I mean, why?"

"Because that was my plan."

"But why now?" Circles under his eyes and brows drawn together, Ted repeatedly rubbed his face.

"I told you before. I was waiting until it was warm enough to take advantage of local outdoor activities."

Ted saw that Summer had already packed her trailer and hooked it to the van. He stood by while she finished putting away final items, then he stammered, "But, but . . . what about Burgundy & Baskets?"

"I'm afraid you'll have to do that one on your own. I've got a date with Bruce Springsteen," she laughed lightly.

"Well," Ted asked, desperate for a positive answer, "are you coming back?"

Summer swallowed hard and said, "No, I think I might head west after that. I wasn't going to leave without saying goodbye. I planned on coming to see you before I took off. But it looks like I've got everything, so . . . I guess this is it," Summer choked.

She approached Ted intending to give him a quick hug, but he latched onto her and held tight.

"Summer, you can't go," he said.

"Ted, I have to go. It's time."

"But what am I going to do without you?" he pled, still holding her.

"You'll be fine. You've got the hang of this thing now."

"But I don't want you to go," Ted said, still clinging to her.

"Ted," Summer said sternly, "you have to let me go."

"But I . . . I . . . " Ted let go of Summer. His eyes welled, and his head dropped in despair. Barely audible, he said, "I'm going to miss you."

"I'm going to miss you, too. We've had a good time. Thank you for that. Goodbye, Ted." Summer darted to the driver's side door. She stepped into the van without looking back and drove away.

Ted watched as the yellow VW bus and tiny trailer turned out of the campground, rumbled down the road, and out of his life.

He returned to his camper, placed his hands on the kitchen table, sunk his head, and wept. He hadn't cried since Carol died. A hollow feeling similar to what he had felt then filled his gut, and he found it difficult to do anything but stare at the nothingness around him.

Slouching, morose, and emotionally depleted, Ted collapsed into his recliner. He silently cursed himself. *I should have told her. Why didn't I tell her how I felt?*

His heart raced. He placed his hands over his face as much to hold back his anger as to hide from the disappointment in himself. Ted slid his hands down the stubble on his cheeks.

I'm a coward! he thought. *All this time, I've been hiding behind the memory of Carol, but in truth, I was just afraid. Scared to take a chance. And now that chance is gone.*

His eyes shot open. *Did she know yesterday that she was leaving today? Did I say something that made her feel like she had to go?* He couldn't think of anything.

Did she plan this? How could she not tell me?

As hurt as he was at the thought, he could not fault Summer.

It was me, all me. I should have fabricated a loophole in the contract. I should have taken the risk.

The older the day grew, the deeper depressed he got. By three o'clock in the afternoon, he had little energy left to think. He drifted into exhaustion, his mind fighting the urge to sleep, his body wanting to give in.

And now she's in Ohio. The thought broke through the sleepy haze.

She's in Ohio. He heard Carol's voice. Then, his own thoughts, *Is this a dream?*

Ted sat upright and jerked his head toward the door, expecting to see Carol standing there. He did not. But he felt her presence, and his heart warmed.

A sense of faith, a new and liberating insight, overrode his knee-jerk reaction to examine the moment so he could determine the origin of the whisper.

Ted shifted his eyes upward and mouthed, "Thank you."

He reached for his cell phone and opened the map app. He checked the distance between Cayuga Lake and the Rock & Roll Hall of Fame.

I can do this, he reasoned. *I need to do this. If I take Route 90, it'll be about a five-hour drive. But I'll have to stop for gas. Maybe add another half hour.*

Ted booted his laptop and searched for the hall of fame website. He took a virtual tour of the building and bought a ticket for the next day.

I'm going to Ohio.

He spent the remainder of late afternoon and evening putting things in their proper place for traveling. He put the outdoor furniture in the SUV and locked it. He disconnected the lights from the motorhome but left them hanging in the campsite. No matter what, he determined, he would need to come back.

He waited until morning before disconnecting the water, sewer, and electric hookups. Ted and his motorhome were on the road to Ohio by eight.

He thought about calling her, but he feared she'd flee to some unknown destination, so he decided against it. Feeling good about his decision, he tried not to think about what could happen once he got there. What if he couldn't find her? But he reasoned he would arrive between one and two in the afternoon, and he had faith that she would still be there.

Traveling Route 90, he passed through Buffalo at 10:15 am. He decided to stop for gas at the Orchard Park exit. Having gone to a couple of football games at the home stadium of New England's premier rival, Ted was familiar with the area.

He stocked up on bottled water and contemplated buying a pre-packaged Danish in the convenience store. He longed for one of Summer's homemade cinnamon buns. He reached for a banana instead.

Back on the road, Ted drove for another hour before a sea of red lights brought traffic to a standstill. In a panic, Ted glanced at the clock. It read 11:56 am.

"Son of a bitch," he exclaimed as he struck the palm of his hand on the steering wheel.

He could not see what caused the stoppage, as several tractor trailers in front of him blocked his view. He had no idea how long the line of vehicles stretched with no exit ahead that he could see.

Stopped, Ted did what he assumed everybody else stopped in the traffic did. He checked his cellphone app to see if he might inch to the next exit and use it as an alternate route. The map app showed him a detour that would add twenty minutes to his trip. He decided to take it if the opportunity arose.

Little by little, traffic inched forward, as did the clock.

What began as frustration soon shifted to anxiety and then fear. Ted knew Summer liked to get an early start to her days. He imagined she would have been waiting at the door of the attraction when it opened at ten. He pictured her slowly wandering the exhibits, sharing memories of the artists with strangers, then lingering with Bruce Springsteen. She would want to leave before they closed at five to avoid sitting in traffic. He reasoned she would leave between three and four.

Inching his motorhome forward, Ted scoffed at his presumptions of Summer, although he knew them correct. *How didn't I realize sooner how important she is to me?*

An accident involving a tractor trailer and an SUV caused the backup. As Ted slowly passed the scene from the far left lane, he saw the truck lying on its side, the cab resting in the breakdown lane, and the trailer lying behind it off the road down a slight incline. The SUV sat in the breakdown lane on a flatbed truck, its front end crushed. Ambulances had come and gone, and crews worked to sweep up the vehicle's debris from the closed right hand and middle lane.

He had lost about an hour but managed to perform a good deed while stopped in traffic. He'd heard a knock on his motorhome door. A pregnant woman desperately in need of a restroom asked to use his. Ted happily obliged. He wished her luck and offered her a bottle of water as she left the RV and returned to a car three vehicles behind.

Still an hour and a half from the Rock & Roll Hall of Fame, Ted estimated he would arrive at 2:30. "Please be there," he whispered. He knew he was cutting it close.

Two miles before his intended exit, Ted's body flooded with nervous excitement. His hands quivered. He lifted his right hand off the wheel and attempted to shake out his anxiety. Then did the same with the left.

Don't you chicken out on me, Ted, he said to himself. As he was about to give himself a pep talk, he saw yellow flashing lights ahead. Construction crews worked on the highway, and traffic was reduced to one lane.

Ted slammed his palm on the steering wheel. "God dammit!"

He watched as hordes of vehicles pulled over into the lane in front of him, keeping him from making headway. His frustration mounted. By the time he cleared the work zone and made it to the exit ramp, Ted had lost another twenty minutes.

The hall of fame stood just off the highway. It was 3:15 pm by the time he pulled into the crowded parking lot. He maneuvered the motorhome like he had been driving it his entire life. He was able to park on the furthest end of the lot, leaving himself a decent hike to the front door. Scanning the parking lot, he did not see Summer's van.

Nearly out of breath and sweating from his hurried walk, he welcomed the air-conditioned venue. He arrived at the main entrance on level one, which brought him to the museum store and café. Crowds of people meandered through the exhibits. *Wow. So many people. How am I going to find her?*

Then Ted recalled his assumption about Summer's visit. He approached a man who appeared to be an employee.

"Excuse me. Could you tell me where to find the Bruce Springsteen exhibit."

After listening to confusing instructions, he made his way to the third level. He wove in and out of the crowd. He stepped up on the edge of an exhibit to scan the area and received an unpleasant glare from a guard. He had no luck. Level three seemed to be the most congested of areas, so he thought he would try Level Five, where he was told he would find something called The Ramp. The employee had said, "If you go to The Ramp, you'll find Bruce Springsteen artifacts in open-air cases." Ted wasn't sure what that meant, but it didn't matter.

He hurriedly searched level five without success. He glanced at his watch. It was nearly four o'clock. An empty bench sat nearby, and Ted took refuge from crowds of people bumping into him. Dejected, he leaned his head back against the wall, closed his eyes, and exhaled.

I blew it. I fucking blew it, he thought. *She's gone.*

Ted didn't open his eyes until he was sure he could keep from tearing up. When he finally gathered the confidence, he stared straight ahead into the crowd gathered in front of him. Then like parting of the sea, people dispersed, some to the right, others to the left to leave her standing alone directly in front of him. She had her back to him, and he thought she looked youthful in jeans and a Bruce Springsteen concert t-shirt. Her gray hair shimmered under the display lights.

Ted's heartbeat quickened. He jumped from the bench and then froze, but his eyes never left her. His feet felt heavy and clumsy, but the longer he watched her, the more he wanted her. His body responded to his intense hunger. If there had been any doubt about how he felt or what he wanted, it had vanished. He found himself moving confidently toward her.

"I think his 1980 Christmas concert in Boston was one of his best," Ted said, standing behind her.

Summer gasped, then quickly turned. "Ted, wh . . . what are you doing here?" she asked, her voice shaky and halted.

"You left before I could tell you something."

"What are you talking about? We said our goodbyes." Her face flushed, and she took a step backwards.

People nearby caught wind of the conversation. Some looked as if they braced for trouble. Others seemed amused.

"I know. But I never should have let you leave without telling you the truth."

"I don't understand," Summer whispered as she eyed the audience that had gathered.

Ted reached for Summer's hands and held them.

"I owe you another apology, Summer."

Summer said, "Ted, maybe we should go somewhere..."

"No," Ted cut her off. "I need to tell you this right now." He cleared his throat, and all those around watched in rapt attention. "I'm sorry. I didn't stick to our deal. I think it's ironic that I, the lawyer, would be the one to break our contract. But here I am."

He paused. "I love you, Summer. I have loved you for some time, but I didn't handle it very well. I love you, and I can't let you leave without knowing it."

A collective gasp rose from the crowd, and all eyes turned to Summer.

Summer pulled her hands from Ted's and placed them over her mouth.

Ted's face grew long. "I'm sorry. I didn't mean to upset you."

Summer placed her hands on Ted's cheeks. "Ted, I love you, too. I love you so much I couldn't stay—because I thought, well, you know ...," Summer said as she glanced at those forming a circle around them. "I broke the contract, too."

Ted let go a heavy sigh. Looking deep into her eyes, he brushed her hair from her face as he caressed her cheek with the back of his hand. He felt her shiver.

He placed his hands lightly on Summer's shoulders and leaned toward her. He kissed her softly and gently. Once, twice.

With the third kiss, they could no longer contain their passion.

He wrapped his arms around her and pulled her to him.

The surrounding crowd cheered and clapped.

"Can we get out of here?" Ted asked.

"Please." Summer blushed as happy tears streaked her cheeks.

They held hands as they quickly made their way to the front entrance, then to the parking lot.

"Come back to the campground where I'm staying," Summer said.

Ted shook his head. "I don't think I can wait that long." He pointed to his motorhome on the other side of the lot.

"Ted, are you crazy?"

"Yes, I am. I'm crazy about you. Besides, think of it as a great adventure." Ted raised a brow.

Summer could not hold back a wide smile. "Let's go."

Walking briskly, Ted and Summer made it to the motorhome and hopped inside. Ted locked the door.

As he headed to the bedroom, Summer said, "Wait."

Ted froze, his face filled with worry.

"You'd better put on some music," Summer said with a playful gaze. "And turn it up loud."

Ted grinned and turned the radio to a classic rock station. Bruce Springsteen's "All the Way Home" sprang from the speakers.

Summer giggled, and Ted embraced her. They shared a strong and passionate kiss.

Ted led her to his bedroom, but just before they stepped inside, he turned to Summer and said, "There's just one more thing."

"What's that, Ted?"

Ted wrapped her in his arms and said, "Call me Teddy."

ONE YEAR LATER

"Let's go, Casey, Frankie. We're going to be late," Marci yelled from Ted's kitchen. "Thanks for watching them last night, Dad. Frank and I had a wonderful date night."

"I'm happy to do it. The boys and I had a great time. Casey is becoming quite a good pool player," Ted grinned.

"Do you want to drive to the baseball game with us?" Marci asked.

"No, thanks. I'll take the Lincoln. I'll see you there."

Casey bounded down the stairs carrying a canvas overnight bag.

"Where's your brother?" Marci asked.

"He's looking for his baseball glove," Casey answered.

"How could he lose his glove? You've only been here for one night." Marci asked.

"We played catch in the backyard," Ted said. "I'll check out there."

Frankie joined them in the kitchen, a concerned look on his face.

"I can't find it," Frankie said, dropping his overnight bag on the floor. He was dressed in his red and white baseball uniform and wore a red cap stitched with a blue letter B.

"Here it is," Ted said as he returned to the kitchen with the glove. "You should take better care of this, Frankie. You left it outside."

"Thanks, Grandpa. I will. Sorry about that." Frankie frowned.

"Boys, go put your stuff in the car," Marci said.

Frankie and Casey raced out the door and to the car.

"Dad, are you all right? You look tired," Marci said.

"I'm fine. It's just been a while since I had to entertain two energetic boys by myself."

"Are you sure that's all? Because I can stay here with you, and Frank can bring the boys on his own."

"Yes, I'm sure! I don't need a babysitter. You worry too much, Marci. You should learn to relax. Maybe you need to meditate more often."

"But . . ."

"Get going. You're going to be late. I'll be there in a little while," Ted said.

Ted sat at the kitchen table. He was tired, and he felt out of sorts. He hadn't slept much in the big, half-empty bed.

A few minutes later, he locked the door behind him as he headed out to the SUV parked alongside his motorhome. He longingly stared at his home away from home, thinking it had sat idle far too long.

He slowly shook his head, and got into the Lincoln, and backed out of the driveway. Bypassing the exit to the baseball field, Ted continued into Boston. A short time later, he pulled into the clinic parking lot. Inside, he walked down the north wing. A familiar figure wearing a white lab coat and a smile stood in the hallway.

"Dan," Ted called.

"Ted? What are you doing here? Doesn't Frankie have a game today?"

"Yes, he does. How is it you know Frankie's game schedule?"

"He's my goddaughter's child. Why wouldn't I know."

"I thought you said you were finally fully retiring."

"I did. I'm just doing a little volunteer work. It keeps me young," Dan smiled. "What brings you here?"

"Me!" Summer said as she approached the two old friends.

Ted and Dan turned to see Summer walking toward them. Ted met her halfway, wrapped her in a hug, and kissed her.

"Hello, Summer. I didn't know you were still here," Dan said.

"She's been here all night," Ted answered, "and I didn't get a wink of sleep." Then he asked Summer, "How did it go?"

"It was a long night, but everything is perfect. Missy Anderson gave birth to a beautiful baby girl at 5:24 this morning. Peter was a trooper. It was one of the happiest moments of my life." Summer's eyes moistened. Ted placed his arm around her and held her close.

"The Andersons? Are they the first of the original group to give birth?" Dan asked.

"They are! But three more children are on their way. We have achieved a seventy-one percent pregnancy rate so far. It's just so amazing." Summer smiled.

"That's an astonishing accomplishment," Dan said.

"I wish it could be one hundred percent," Summer mused, "but we don't live in a perfect world. And you, Dan, are a big part of this. I can't thank you enough for all the time you donate. You were here so late last night. Why are you back already?"

Ted raised an eyebrow. "So much for being retired."

Dan ignored Ted's comment.

"I had a few patients to check on. I was just getting ready to leave."

"Do you want to drive to the game with us?" Summer asked Dan.

"Son of a softball," Ted said. "Summer told you last night that Frankie had a game today. He's my goddaughter's child, my eye!"

Dan laughed at his foiled deception.

"I'll take my own car, thanks. I've got a date after the game," Dan grinned.

"With what, an ice cream?" Ted asked.

"No," Dan said. "With a very attractive doctor. I'm taking her to Donatello's for an early dinner."

"Eve? Are you dating Dr. Fellows? She's wonderful. She and I were just talking about you. Of course, I didn't know it was you we were talking about," Summer confessed. "She seemed very excited about tonight. I hope you two have a fantastic evening. But right now, we better get going or we're going to miss the whole first inning." Summer gazed at Ted.

"See you at the game, Dan," Ted called over his shoulder as he and Summer headed down the hall.

In the car, Summer sat back and sighed. "I wish you could have been there. It was magical. She is the sweetest little baby. And you'll never guess what they named her."

"Summer?" Ted asked.

"No. Autumn," Summer chuckled.

The grass still hung onto the morning dew when the teams took to the field. It was a competitive game, but Frankie's team won by a single run. Frankie made the final out from shortstop by diving for a line drive. Ted beamed as they walked to the parking lot.

"You had quite a night!" Ted remarked to Summer after they said their goodbyes to Marci, Frank, and the boys.

"I'm exhausted and exhilarated. Missy insisted I stay in the room with her during delivery. Ted, I've never felt anything like that in my life," Summer said with tears in her eyes.

"You are an amazing person, Summer. Have you stopped to think about what you've done for these families? Autumn Anderson is here because of you!"

"Autumn is here because of the fleet of doctors, nurses, technicians, and everybody else who works so tirelessly. I just provided the building."

"That's not true, and I know, deep down, you know it isn't. You and Arnold have a lot to be proud of, and that clinic is a life changer. I'm so proud of you."

"All right, Teddy, enough." Summer reached from her seat and gave him a light slap on his arm. "Are you trying to make me fall apart?" She chuckled.

After a few moments, Ted said, "I've been thinking. What do you say we hop in the motorhome tomorrow and go for a ride?"

"All right! Where do you want to go?" Summer asked.

"How about the Grand Canyon?"

"The Grand Canyon? I thought you were going to say Vermont or Maine."

"Don't you want to go to the Grand Canyon?"

"Of course, I do. We've talked about it, but we never said when we would go. We need to plan . . . " Summer stopped midsentence, then asked, "How long have you been researching the trip, Teddy?"

"I haven't. In fact, it just kind of came out of my mouth. I was thinking we should take a trip. I hadn't thought about where until you asked. But I like the idea," Ted grinned.

"And you want to go tomorrow?"

"Yes, I do."

"Well, I'll be a son of a duck!"

ACKNOWLEDGEMENTS

I am thankful for incredible support and encouragement I receive from friends, family, devoted readers, and spirit guides.

A novel does not get to print without the help of a lot of people. The first person to lay eyes on this manuscript was my developmental editor, Rozi Doci. I thank her for sharing her expertise and pushing me in the right direction.

Thank you to Richard Bruno for proofreading *Winter Meets Summer*. We all know how catastrophic it can be to have a comma in the wrong place.

To my pre-readers—Paula Francis, Mary Johnson, Pamela Johnson, and Brenda Anderson—thank you for your input, honesty, and support.

To my social media friends, the cover of this book is dedicated to you. It seems I have a host of talented graphic artists on my side.

And finally, to my friend, editor, and publisher, Marcia Gagliardi—we make a great team, and I am forever grateful you walked into my store that life-changing day.

ABOUT the AUTHOR

You can't always plan where life will take you.

That certainly proved true for Christine Noyes. Growing up a tomboy in Shrewsbury, Massachusetts, she spent her youth building forts, playing sports, and enjoying the perceived innocence of the 1960s.

Without a clear vision of what her life should be, she went where she felt most comfortable: to the kitchen. At the age of eleven, she began her work life as a dishwasher in her grandfather's restaurant. She spent the next several decades reinventing herself, becoming an accomplished chef and then a sales representative, an entrepreneur, and eventually a writer and illustrator.

Chris never chose her professions. They chose her.

Few people say that going bowling changed their lives, but it did exactly that for Chris. She met the one person she never expected to meet, the man she calls her husband and soulmate, Al.

COLOPHON

MVB Verdigris is a Garalde text family for the digital age. Inspired by work of sixteenth-century punchcutters Robert Granjon, Hendrik van den Keere, and Pierre Haultin, MVB Verdigris celebrates tradition but is not beholden to it. Created to deliver good typographic color as text, Mark van Bronkhorst's design meets the needs of today's designer using today's paper and press. A full-featured OpenType release with an added titling companion, it's optimized for the latest typesetting technologies too.

Garalde: the word itself sounds antique and arcane to anyone who isn't fresh out of design school, but the sort of typeface it describes is actually quite familiar to all of us. Despite its age—born fairly early in printing's history—the style has fared well. Garaldes are the typefaces of choice for books and other long reading. And so we continue to see text set in old favorites—Garamond, Sabon, and their Venetian predecessor, Bembo. Yet many new books don't feel as handsome and readable as older books printed in the original, metal type. The problem is that digital type revivals are typically facsimiles of their metal predecessors, merely duplicating the letterforms rather than capturing the impression—both physical and emotional—that the typefaces once left on the page.